no
means no

kathy lee

D1428835

Copyright © Kathy Lee 2007
First published 2007
ISBN 978 184427 2532

Scripture Union
207–209 Queensway, Bletchley, Milton Keynes, MK2 2EB, England
Email: info@scriptureunion.org.uk
Website: www.scriptureunion.org.uk

Scripture Union Australia
Locked Bag 2, Central Coast Business Centre, NSW 2252
Website: www.scriptureunion.org.au

Scripture Union USA
PO Box 987, Valley Forge, PA 19482
Website: www.scriptureunion.org

British Library Cataloguing-in-Publication Data.
A catalogue record of this book is available from the British Library.

Printed in the UK by CPI Bookmarque, Croydon, CR0 4TD

Cover design by Pink Cabana
Internal design and layout by Author & Publisher Services

☙ Scripture Union is an international Christian charity working with churches in more than 130 countries, providing resources to bring the good news about Jesus Christ to children, young people and families and to encourage them to develop spiritually through the Bible and prayer.

As well as our network of volunteers, staff and associates who run holidays, church-based events and school Christian groups, we produce a wide range of publications and support those who use our resources through training programmes.

Contents

1

Problem parents

Abena and I were round at Charlie's, trying out some new eye make-up. Looking at the result in the mirror, I groaned.

'Why do I still keep hoping that things will actually do what they promise in the ads?'

Abena inspected me critically. 'You know, your eyelashes do look longer and thicker, just like it says.'

'Yes, but that doesn't make me look like the model in the picture. That's what I paid £8.95 for. I was robbed!'

Actually, none of us looks much like a model. We don't have endless legs, enormous eyes or razor-sharp cheekbones. Abena may grow tall enough to become the next black supermodel, but she'll never be stick thin. And Charlie's slim enough, I suppose, but her face is nothing special. As for me, you could say I'm reasonable-looking, but not startlingly beautiful. I have grey eyes and shoulder-length, light-brown hair.

Charlie was looking at herself in the mirror. My black mascara looked completely wrong with her pale, red-gold eyebrows and fair, freckled skin. 'Oh, yuck,' she said. 'Like two spiders sitting on my eyelids.'

Maybe her eyes aren't her best feature, but at least she doesn't have my problem. Ever since I was born, I've had a slight squint. I have to wear glasses to help correct it, and I hate them. They're so old-fashioned –

like something out of an ancient movie. You know the kind of thing. The plain girl in thick glasses is totally transformed when she takes them off, becoming a gorgeous, irresistible, all-singing, all-dancing heroine.

Exactly the same thing happened to me when I took off those horrible glasses for the first time. (Okay, not *exactly* the same. For some reason I didn't start tap-dancing around the room.) Even though I still have to wear the seriously uncool clothes Mum buys for me, I'm a lot better-looking without my glasses, and far more confident. Whenever I'm in school now, I take them off. Obviously I still have to wear them anywhere within range of Mum – she'd go mad if she realised what I was doing.

But after a few hours without glasses, I often get a terrible headache. I have no choice then – I've got to put them back on.

It was starting to happen now. (The warning sign is when I begin seeing two of everything.) With a sigh, I dug my glasses out of my bag. To disguise them, I kept them in a Gucci case I got from a charity shop. But nothing could disguise how awful they were when I actually put them on.

I looked in the mirror again. I might as well not have bothered putting on any eye make-up. No one would notice it now… all they would see would be my glasses.

If only I could have some more designer-looking frames, ones that suited my face, it wouldn't be so bad. I'd seen some I liked in an optician's, and I'd told Mum about them.

'How much were they?' she'd asked.

This was the bit I'd been afraid of.

'£230,' I'd muttered.

'*How* much?'

'£230.'

'I'm sorry, Eunice. We can't possibly afford them at the moment. Moving was expensive, you know. And there's nothing wrong with the glasses you already have.'

'But Mum! They make me look terrible!'

'No they don't,' she'd said. 'You're being silly. You look perfectly all right in them.'

This wasn't reassuring, coming from Mum. She had as much interest in fashion as a snake might have in playing the saxophone. She was quite happy wearing old clothes from jumble sales, and her hairstyle was exactly the same as in her wedding photo of 30 years ago (except much greyer).

She'd said, 'In any case, you won't have to wear those glasses for ever. In another few years, you might have that operation the specialist talked about.'

'In another few *years*? So I have to go on looking terrible for years?'

'You look fine, dear. Don't get so worked up about it.'

I wondered if Mum actually wanted me to be the kind of person boys don't notice. In her opinion I was far too young to be thinking about boys. (She had never had a boyfriend until she was 18, when she met my dad.)

'Mum, if you get me some decent glasses, I won't ask for any pocket money for a whole year.'

'I said no, Eunice. No means no.'

When she'd said that, I knew it was no good going on about it. I would only make her angry.

****

My parents are my biggest problem in life. For a start, there's Dad's work – he's a vicar. People seem to expect a vicar to be better than everyone else... always kind, polite and good-tempered. And his family should be the same. It's very hard to live up to. And that's if you *want* to live up to it in the first place – which I don't.

Then there's the fact that Mum and Dad are so old. I'm 13; they're 53, old enough to be my grandparents. They have old-fashioned ideas about everything. They even gave me an old-fashioned name, Eunice, after a woman in the Bible.

They were married for 18 years before I came along. They had got used to the idea that they would never have children, although Mum said she always felt sad about it. And then, after years of longing and praying, she found she was expecting a baby. Me.

So I suppose it's natural that she worries a lot. But all her hopes and fears seem to wrap tightly around me like clothes that are too small. I can't breathe properly. I can't stretch and grow.

When we moved to the city last year, after ten years in a country village, I decided to change my name. At my new school, I got people to call me Emma, which is my middle name. I was tired of being Eunice, the vicar's daughter – such a good little girl, quiet and serious. Boring, in other words.

Emma wasn't like that. Emma was easy to get on with, a bit of a laugh. Anyway, that's what I was like in school and with my friends. But whenever I went home, something happened. Like a magic spell, just walking through the door turned me into Eunice again. It's hard to be different from what people expect you to be.

I did start to do something new – discussing things more with Mum and Dad. Well, I called it discussing; Mum called it arguing, and she didn't like it. She was used to having a daughter who accepted whatever she was told.

Dad didn't mind so much. 'It shows she's growing up,' I heard him say to Mum. 'Developing ideas of her own. And that's good, don't you think?'

'Mmmm.' I could tell she wasn't convinced.

****

'How am I going to get enough money to buy those glasses?' I asked my friends.

'You could get a Saturday job,' Charlie suggested.

'Yeah, like what?' Abena asked.

'I dunno. Shop assistant or something.'

'They all want you to be 16,' said Abena. 'The only thing they'll let you do at our age is a paper round.'

I said, 'My parents would never agree to that. Out alone, early on a dark winter morning – never. They'd be certain I would get abducted by evil strangers.'

Actually I had no desire to do a paper round. I have enough trouble getting up in the mornings as it is.

'What about babysitting, then?' Charlie asked.

'Mmm... trouble is I don't know much about young kids. Remember, I haven't got any brothers or sisters.'

'But it's easy,' said Abena. 'I babysit for our neighbour sometimes, and I never have to do much. The kids are in bed. All I have to do is make sure they stay there. Then they go to sleep, and I sit there watching TV and getting paid for it.'

'No nappy changing?' I said. 'No screaming babies?'

'I suppose that depends on who you babysit for,' said Charlie. 'You could tell people you can't look after anyone younger than 2.'

'Or older than about 10, when they start getting cheeky,' said Abena.

I thought about this. Although I didn't particularly like young children, I might manage to put up with them for a few hours, if I was getting paid enough. It would be worth a try, anyway.

'Maybe I could advertise in the church newsletter,' I said.

The others thought this was an excellent idea. 'And if you get lots of replies – more than you need – pass them on to me,' said Abena.

Charlie said, 'Or me. We could start our own babysitting service! I could really do with the money.'

We were all starting to get enthusiastic. Charlie began planning how to spend all the money she would make. But then I faced a reality check.

'I don't know if my parents will let me do it.'

'Oh, Emma. You always say that.' Charlie sounded impatient. 'I think it's just an excuse when you don't want to do something.'

'That's not true! You know what my mum's like. She'll find some reason to stop me – it will interfere with my homework or something.'

'Don't give up hope before you've even asked her,' said Abena.

'I will ask her. I'll do it tonight. But don't say I didn't warn you.'

2
What would people say?

'Well…' Mum said, looking thoughtful, 'we'd better see what your father says.'

At least she didn't come straight out with 'No means no'. But I could see she wasn't all that keen on the babysitting plan.

'The thing that worries me is, what would you do if something went wrong?' she said. 'Suppose a child was ill, or had an accident? Or simply started being naughty? It's quite a responsibility looking after children, you know.'

'I'm nearly 14,' I reminded her. 'The same age as Abena, and she's been looking after her neighbour's kids for ages.'

Mum ignored this. 'And you're talking about advertising in the parish newsletter. In one way, that's a good idea – you'd be working for church members, people we know. But if anything *did* go wrong, the whole parish would know about it. What would people think?'

That's something Mum has always worried about, ever since I can remember. *What will people think? What will they say about us? As Christians, we have standards to keep, especially since Dad is a vicar. We mustn't give people anything to complain about.*

This was the reason she got so upset over the Rachel/Mark business. She hated the fact that I was involved in it – what on earth would people say? The vicar's daughter causing trouble and lying to her own parents!

Rachel was a girl I met soon after we moved to Birton. Her family belonged to the church. She was blonde, beautiful and boy-mad. The trouble began when she got keen on Mark, who helped to run the church youth group. Mark wasn't interested, and Rachel – who wasn't used to being turned down – was furious. Rachel told all kinds of lies about Mark, expecting Charlie and me to back her up. She actually got Mark suspended from his job.

In the end, Charlie told Dad what had really happened (nothing). But Rachel stuck to her story, and the whole thing had to be investigated. The after-effects are still going on, like the aftershocks of an earthquake. Rachel's been moved to a different school, and her family have stopped coming to St Jude's. From things I'd heard Dad say, I knew that they weren't happy with the way the situation had been handled. They believed every word Rachel said... which proved they didn't know their own daughter too well.

Sometimes I felt glad that Rachel wasn't around any more. Other times, I missed her. She certainly used to liven things up.

By now, it was the end of our first week in Year 9. Charlie, Abena and I were at the same school, in different classes. But we discovered that most of our teachers were saying exactly the same sort of things. *Start as you mean to go on… get your homework in on time… take things seriously… blah, blah, blah.*

Rachel, where are you now that we need you?

****

Luckily, when I asked him, Dad approved of the babysitting idea. He even helped me put together an advert for the church newsletter.

> *Don't miss that special event*
> *because you can't find a babysitter!*
> *Teenage girls from St Jude's youth group*
> *have started a babysitting service.*
> *Call 352568 to find out more.*

Mum liked the ad because it didn't give my name. Also, the phone number was for our home phone, which meant she might be able to keep an eye on things. The church youth group was mentioned – this was my idea – to make people think we were honest, reliable, well-behaved and so on.

On Sunday, when the advert appeared, I pointed it out to Charlie and Abena.

'Why didn't you put in our mobile numbers?' said Abena.

'Dad wouldn't let me. He said we might start getting strange phone calls.'

'What's this about babysitting?' someone asked Mary, the leader in charge of the Sunday night youth group known as The Garret (although it actually meets in the church hall, not in the loft).

'You'd better ask Charlie or Abena or Eunice,' Mary said. (Eunice – yes, I'm still called Eunice at youth group, and I have to wear my Eunice-type clothes. This is annoying because there are several boys at The Garret who are worth a second look, but none of them has even glanced in my direction.)

We explained what we were doing.

Joe said, 'If I had kids I wouldn't give them to you to look after.'

Joe is one of the good-looking boys – and he knows it. He seems to think he can be quite mean to girls and they'll still love him. Not Charlie, though. She said, 'If you had kids I wouldn't go within a mile of them. Even for £20 an hour.'

Harry, Joe's friend, butted in. 'Your advert's illegal. It's blatantly sexist. Boys can babysit as well as girls, can't they?'

'There's nothing to stop you setting up your own babysitting service,' said Abena.

I said, 'Except that no one will book you.'

'Oh yeah? You almost make me want to try it, just to prove you're wrong,' said Harry. 'Only problem is, I can't stand kids.'

'So? You don't have to like them,' said Abena. 'If you try to be all nice to them and be their friend, they won't do a thing you say. I learned that the hard way.'

I noticed Charlie had been keeping very quiet since Harry arrived. This was a big give-away – she liked him, although I couldn't see why. He was nothing much to look at; there were far better-looking boys at the club. My favourite was Jayesh, who was Indian, with film-star looks and jet black hair.

What would Mum say if I had an Indian boyfriend? Somehow I knew she wouldn't be too keen. (Actually, she wouldn't like me having a boyfriend, full stop.) Mum couldn't get used to the multicultural life of the city. To her, normal life was our old village, where absolutely everyone was English born and bred. The only 'foreigners' were the vet and his wife, from Glasgow.

But I liked my new life. It was a lot more interesting. I liked the fact that at school we had people from over 20 different countries, some of them still struggling to speak English. (This included a couple of the teachers.) I liked the local market, with its huge variety of stalls – saris alongside jeans, halal meat opposite burgers, plantains and yams next to apples and pears.

In our area, as well as various churches, there was a mosque and a Sikh temple. At school I heard about different festivals – Ramadan and Diwali and Hanukkah – not in RE lessons, but as part of people's lives. It made me think.

Naturally, I had been brought up believing in God – the Christian god. All the other gods that people worshipped, all over the world, were just cheap imitations. Mistakes. Idols. But how could Christians be so sure of that?

My RE teacher said that perhaps every religion led to the same place in the end. All had some truth in them. I found that hard to believe, because the gods were so different from one another, and they wanted different things from people. Which was the true God, or gods?

Maybe there was no God at all. This would mean that Dad's whole life had been a bit of a waste – serving someone who didn't exist. Well, not a waste exactly, since it seemed to have made him happy. But it didn't make *me* happy. My life would be a whole lot easier if God didn't exist.

When I discussed this with Charlie, I found she was thinking along the same lines. She didn't really believe in God, although she often came to church with her mum, and never missed a Sunday night at The Garret.

She said, 'Maybe there is a God, maybe there isn't. Sometimes I think there is – like when people's prayers get answered.'

'A lot of prayers *don't* get answered, though,' I said. 'It could just be luck.'

'What I figure is, I've got plenty of time. When I'm as old as my mum, I might start believing in God. Not yet, though. At the moment I want to enjoy myself.'

I decided not to talk to Abena about my thoughts. From the stuff she says, it sounds like God is really important to her. She would probably try to persuade me that I was wrong – that God did exist and I ought to follow him. I didn't want to hear that.

And I didn't listen to the small voice that sometimes spoke to me. It was like a feeling nudging me towards doing or saying something. (Or, sometimes, maybe *not* doing something.) God's voice? Or just my conscience, a result of brainwashing by my parents when I was young? Whatever it was, I ignored it.

From now on, I was going to do as I pleased. I would live my life obeying not God, nor my parents, but only myself.

Naturally I didn't tell Mum and Dad about this decision. It would only upset them.

3

The stranger

We got our first response to the babysitting ad within a couple of days. It was from a family with four young children. Four! They wanted a sitter for Saturday night.

Now we faced a problem. How should we decide which person took on which job? It wouldn't be fair if Abena, the most experienced person, always got the tricky ones.

'The fairest thing would be to take turns,' said Charlie. 'We can throw dice to see who gets the first go.'

The dice gave me two sixes. Noticing my look of horror, Abena said, 'I could come with you to begin with, until you get used to it.'

'Would you really?' I said gratefully. 'If you do, I'll give you half the money.'

When we turned up on the Gibsons' doorstep, Mrs Gibson looked taken aback, and she asked how old we were.

'Thirteen? I suppose I should have checked beforehand... You're only three years older than Chloe, my eldest.'

'There are two of us,' I pointed out. 'That gives us a combined age of 26. And Abena's done loads of babysitting.'

'And we'll call you at once if there are any problems,' Abena reassured her. 'It'll be fine – really.'

It was fine. The four of them were all good kids, and the eldest two, who were still up, went to bed as soon as we told them it was time. The Gibsons came back at 11.30 to find everything in perfect order. The kids had even put away some of their toys, so the living room looked tidier than when we'd arrived.

Mr Gibson gave us a lift home, paid us, and assured us that he would call us again soon.

'See? It's a doddle,' said Abena.

'If we could do this every night of the week, we'd make a fortune,' I said.

Unfortunately, it was mostly at weekends that people needed a sitter – during the week there wasn't much to do. Also, not all children were as good as the Gibsons.

After two or three more jobs with Abena holding my hand, I decided I was confident enough to go it alone. The next job was to look after a 4-year-old called Molly. Just one child, aged 4… I ought to be able to manage that.

The trouble with Molly was, she didn't want to stay in bed. She came downstairs about a dozen times, each time with a different excuse. Thirsty… hungry… too hot… too cold… lost her toy tiger… thirsty again…

I found out what Abena had meant about not being too nice. The only way to make Molly stay in bed was to yell at her. But I overdid it a bit. Looking terrified, she ran upstairs and hid under the bed.

I couldn't persuade her to come out. She just lay there, whimpering. When I tried to grab her arm and pull her out, the whimpers changed to terrified screams. Oh, help... what if she was still under there when her parents came back?

I didn't want to ring Abena, because that would mean admitting I was a failure. But in the end I had to.

I will never have a better friend than Abena. She came round straight away. And she didn't laugh or make me feel stupid – she just solved the problem.

'Has Molly got a favourite toy?' she asked me.

'How am I supposed to know? Oh, hold on a minute... there was this fluffy tiger...'

Abena found the toy under Molly's pillow. Holding it where the kid could see it, she almost managed to persuade her to come out. But as soon as Molly saw me, she ducked back into her hiding-place.

'I don't like her,' she whined. 'Make her go away.'

'Sure. Your tiger will chase her away,' said Abena. Growling loudly, she made the tiger leap at me. I got the idea. I screamed and ran out of the room.

'Okay, you can come out now,' I heard her telling Molly.

Ten minutes later, Molly was fast asleep in bed. She looked calm, peaceful and angelic.

'I owe you for this. Big time,' I told Abena. 'How did you know what to do?'

'Years of practice on my little brother. I hated it at the time. I never knew it would turn out to be useful.'

'You should write a beginner's guide to babysitting. Like, Rule 1 – don't be too nice. Rule 2 – don't be too nasty.'

Abena laughed. 'Rule 3 – find out what the child's favourite toy is. NB. This may not be so useful if it's a Playstation or a Lego pirate ship.'

'Rule 4 – don't feel the need to tell the parents every little detail of the evening,' I said. 'I wonder if Molly will say anything about what happened?'

But she can't have, because Molly's mum asked us to sit for her again. We decided I'd better not be the one to do it. Abena could have that pleasure.

****

Living in a vicarage, I was used to people calling round, or ringing up at all kinds of times – day and night. They usually wanted Dad, and they seemed to think he should be available 24/7. If he was out visiting, or attending a meeting, they sometimes got annoyed. Mum had taught me always to be polite to people, even if they didn't deserve it.

But when the hooded stranger came to the door, she broke her own rules.

I was doing my homework when I suddenly heard the sound of raised voices. Or rather, one raised voice, sounding high and nervous – not like Mum at all.

'No! I've just told you, he isn't here! Now go away. You can't come in.'

Feeling curious, I got up and went into the hall. The front door was open, and a cold draught blew in from the darkness. A stranger was standing on the doorstep. Under the shadow of his hoodie, his face was pale and desperate-looking.

'Please,' he said, in a slurred, hoarse voice. 'I'm homeless. I've got nowhere to go and no money.'

Mum's politeness came to the surface again. 'I'm sorry, but you can't come in. Come back tomorrow, when my husband will be here.'

She began to close the door. At the same moment, the stranger lurched forward. Mum cried out and struggled to push the door shut, but the man's foot was in the way. His face, half-seen in the gap of the door, looked twisted and ugly, hardly human, like a Halloween mask.

'Get out! I'll call the police!' Mum gasped.

I ran towards the phone on the hall table. Was it any use? Could the police come in time? Suppose the man had a knife...

'Eunice! Let the dogs out!' Mum shouted. Of course there were no dogs. But the stranger didn't know that. Just for a second, he hesitated.

I made for the kitchen, calling, 'Here, Tyson! Here, Spike!' Before I had time to wonder what to do next (start barking?) I heard the front door slam shut. Mum was leaning against it, looking as if she was about to collapse.

'The back door – is it locked?' she managed to say.

I checked it. Then I peered out between the curtains of the front window, half-expecting to see that pale, frightening face pressed against the glass.

But it was all right. Dark under the orange glow of the lights, the stranger was walking slowly away. His head was bent, his shoulders hunched.

'He's gone,' I told Mum.

'Oh, thank God…' She sank down on the sofa.

'That was scary,' I said. 'Was he drunk?'

'Either drunk or on drugs. His eyes looked quite strange… But I shouldn't have panicked like that. It wouldn't have been so bad if your father had been there.'

I wondered what Dad could have done against a drug-crazed stranger, 30 years younger than he was. Not a lot, probably.

Mum said, 'This kind of thing simply didn't happen in Nembury. I wish…'

Then she stopped. *I wish we'd stayed there* – was that what she'd been about to say? But she would never admit that. She always backed Dad up in whatever he did.

'You wish what, Mum?'

'I wish you'd make me a cup of tea, dear.' She smiled faintly. 'That might make me feel better.'

****

Two things happened after that. One: we always used the security chain when we answered the door at night. Two: Dad got interested in homeless people and their problems. Quite a few of them lived in the parish, sleeping rough under the railway arches by the industrial estate.

Dad said they were just as much his responsibility as the other people in his parish, the ones fortunate enough to have homes to live in. Sometimes he would stop and talk to a homeless person, or buy them some food. He didn't like to give money, because it might be spent on drink or drugs.

'Do you know,' he said to Mum, 'there's absolutely nowhere for homeless people to go in this area. There used to be a council drop-in centre where they could go in the daytime, but it's been closed down to save money. Now there's nothing.'

Mum looked at him. 'You're planning something, Giles. I know that tone of voice.'

'Well, I can't help thinking that our parish hall is rather underused. The young people have it on Sunday evenings, and the ladies' group meets there on Wednesdays, but apart from that it's empty most of the time. I would love to see it being used as a place where homeless people could just call in and feel welcome. A hot drink, maybe a meal... perhaps we could have a store of second-hand clothes to give out...'

'The neighbours would absolutely hate the idea,' said Mum.

By 'neighbours', she meant the people who lived in Church Street. Very few of them ever came to church, except to complain about things: cars parking on a Sunday morning, noisy kids leaving the youth group at night, bell-ringing, music... you name it, they moaned about it.

Mum was right – the neighbours wouldn't like the idea of a centre for homeless people starting up here, in their quiet street.

'Well, perhaps we can persuade them,' Dad said mildly. 'Do *you* think it's a good idea, Marjorie?'

Mum hesitated, and I could see that she wasn't too keen. Neither was I. The word 'homeless' instantly brought to mind that man at the door.

All right, so not all homeless people were like our strange visitor. Some, as Dad pointed out, weren't much older than me. But why didn't they get their lives sorted? They shouldn't hang around making the place look untidy. And most of them *smelled*.

'Well?' Dad asked Mum. 'Should I go ahead with this? I feel it could be God's calling for us in this parish.'

'Whatever you think, dear,' she said, and turned away.

4

Lost causes

Dad didn't seem to notice our lack of enthusiasm. He mentioned his idea in a sermon the very next week. It was one of his better sermons. People were really listening, not nodding off as they sometimes did.

They either liked the idea or hated it. You could see it in their faces. (A few looked undecided. Probably they hated it and yet thought they *ought* to like it, because after all, Christians are supposed to help the poor and the homeless. But couldn't they do it by sending a donation somewhere?)

'St Jude, our patron saint, is sometimes called the saint of lost causes or desperate situations,' Dad said. 'Many homeless people are in a desperate situation. Many of them feel lost. We could reach out a hand to them in God's name, and show them his love. But it wouldn't be an easy thing to do. We would be doing what God does – loving the people who are hardest to love. The ones with problems. The ones most people cross the road to avoid.'

When I asked my friends later on, I was surprised to find that they thought Dad's idea was a good one. But then I remembered about Zack, Charlie's brother. Zack had run away a few weeks before. All we knew was that he was somewhere on the south coast – possibly homeless himself.

'Maybe if I do something to help a homeless person here,' Charlie said, 'somebody else will do the same for Zack.'

'You'd actually be prepared to help with this?' I said.

'Yeah, why not?'

'I would, too,' said Abena.

'I knew *you* would,' I said. 'Saint Abena.'

We were hanging around in the church hall, waiting for youth group to start.

Charlie said, 'I never knew St Jude was the saint of... what was it? Lost causes, desperate situations? Wonder if he could help with my maths homework.'

'Or get Harry to ask you out,' Abena suggested.

'Shut up,' said Charlie fiercely, although Harry was on the opposite side of the room.

'He can't possibly hear you unless he's got ears like a bat's,' said Abena.

I said, 'He does have ears like bats. Table tennis bats.'

Charlie scowled at me, her face pink.

Suddenly I noticed that there was a silence in the room. Everyone was looking towards the door. I turned to see who had just come in.

It was Mark. He had been suspended from being a youth leader while Rachel's accusations were being checked out. Now it looked as if he was being allowed back.

He was acting cool and calm, as if he'd never been away. Everyone was pleased to see him. After they got over their surprise, people practically mobbed him.

'I'm glad he's back,' said Abena. 'He has good ideas for the club. I wonder if he'll organise a Christmas party, like last year.'

I looked at Charlie, and I could tell she was feeling the same as me... not exactly pleased to see Mark. Probably, like me, she felt guilty. What would he say to us?

But we needn't have worried. Mark seemed to have done the Christian thing, and forgiven us. He treated Charlie and me exactly the same as everyone else – almost as if he'd forgotten the whole Rachel episode.

I knew he hadn't forgotten, though. My parents certainly hadn't. My mum was a lot more suspicious of me than she used to be – checking up that I really was where I said I was, and insisting on picking me up afterwards, as if I was a little kid.

When I told people at school what she was like, they couldn't believe it. She was far stricter than anyone else's mother.

'She wouldn't let you see *Witch Hunt*?' said Sophie, disbelieving. 'But it's only a 12. My kid sister's seen it.'

I said, 'She won't let me go to parties. She won't let me buy my own clothes, even with my own money that I earned myself.'

'Why not?' asked Bindi.

'In case I buy something that's a little bit too short or too tight or too sexy.'

Sophie giggled. 'Not like what you're wearing now.'

'Well, Mum never sees me like this.'

I was in school uniform, of course, but I'd turned the waistband over a couple of times to make the skirt shorter, and undone the top buttons of the shirt. I had also untied my hair from its neat ponytail, put some lip gloss on, and taken off my glasses. At the start of each day I went into the girls' toilets looking like Eunice, and came out again as Emma. I had to reverse the process at the end of the day, before Mum saw me.

'You're like a spy in a film,' said Bindi. 'You have a secret identity.'

'Which is the real you?' Sophie asked.

'This is the real me. When I go home – that's when I'm pretending to be someone else.'

'Weird,' said Bindi.

Sophie said, 'You can't go on pretending for ever. You should stand up to your mum. I mean, not letting you buy your own clothes! She must be some kind of control freak. Is she still going to be choosing your clothes for you when you're 18?'

When she put it like that, I saw that I had to do something. There was a party coming up, and – amazingly – Mum had agreed to let me go. (It was being given by a girl from youth group, and her mother was guaranteed to be there throughout the evening.) I wanted to wear something really great, something non-Eunice, so that the boys would notice me for a change.

But how? I would need to: (a) go on a secret shopping trip, (b) hide my new clothes from Mum,

(c) get to the party without her seeing what I was wearing. Difficult, but not impossible.

I started making plans. And then, one evening, my mobile phone rang. It was a number I didn't recognise. But I knew the voice instantly, although I hadn't heard it for months.

'Hi, Emma. How's things?'

It was the last person in the world I expected to hear from – Rachel.

5

A bit of excitement

'Things are OK,' I said cautiously. 'How about you?'

'Not too good. I can't stand Highfield School, and I hate old Greta – that's our housekeeper, or rather prison warder. I was just sitting here thinking about the good old days with you and Charlie and Abena, and I thought, I may not be allowed to see you any more, but at least I could ring you.'

'*You're* not allowed to see *us*?'

'No. My mum and dad think you led me astray.' She laughed, because she was the one who'd done most of the leading. She was always the one with the ideas and the nerve (some people would call it idiocy) to try them out.

I wondered why she'd chosen me as the person to ring. After all, she'd known Charlie and Abena much longer than me. I felt flattered.

'Nice to hear from you,' I said. 'We miss you. Life is a lot more boring without you.'

'You think you're bored? You should try a week at Highfield. It's the most boring school in the entire universe. People are already worried about their GCSEs, and we're only in Year 9. I mean, lighten up a bit! Get a life!'

She started telling me all about the school – the strict rules, the awful uniform, the piles and piles of homework, and worst of all, the lack of boys. It was an all-girls school.

'And they're all so bitchy,' she said. 'They've got their own little groups, and they make you feel totally left out. There's me and this other new girl – we hang around together because the others hardly speak to us. I can't tell you how awful it is! Look, Emma, can you call me back? I'm running out of credit. My parents are being so mean with money these days.'

I called her, but I was pretty low on credit myself, and I didn't dare use the house phone in case Mum realised who I was talking to. (She doesn't exactly listen in on my calls. She just happens to pass through the hall rather a lot when I'm on the phone.)

'We could meet up,' Rachel suggested.

'Like when?'

'Wednesday morning any good? It's my worst morning of an awful week.'

'You mean, bunk off school? But you said they're ultra-strict. Won't they notice?'

'Not if I'm back in time for afternoon registration. If we're going to meet, it will have to be in school hours, because Greta picks me up after school.'

I knew there would be no problem at my school, where people bunked off all the time. Unless they missed an entire half-term, nothing much seemed to be done about it. But I had never tried it. The thought made me feel nervous.

'Oh, come on,' said Rachel. 'It'll be a laugh. We could meet up in the centre of town and go shopping... like we used to.'

'Shopping! Good idea. You can help me buy some clothes my mum wouldn't like.'

We agreed to meet at the city-centre bus station. There were loos there where Rachel could change out of her uniform. It was an old-fashioned brown pinafore dress with a gold logo, unmistakably marking her out as a Highfield girl. (Again, not a problem for me. All I had to do was take off my school tie and I could merge with the crowd.)

'Okay, see you on Wednesday then.'

I wondered whether to tell Charlie and Abena, but in the end I decided not to. After all, Rachel had called me, not them. Also, Abena might try to persuade me not to go. Rachel hadn't been too nice to Abena at the end of last term.

And I wanted to go. By now I was looking forward to it.

****

It was easy to slip out of school after registration on Wednesday morning. If anyone challenged me, I was going to say I had a dentist's appointment, but no one said a word. On the bus, I took off my tie and slid it into my bag, ignoring a disapproving glance from an old woman. 'Shouldn't you be in school?' she was obviously dying to say.

The feeling of freedom was great. I should be in school doing History and English and Games (horrible hockey or nightmare netball). Instead I was heading for the city centre, and no one could stop me! Yes!

I was just another face among thousands – that was the real freedom. It wasn't like my old life in the village, where everyone knew me. 'That's Eunice, the vicar's daughter. Why isn't she in school? Not playing truant, is she? I'd better have a word with her mother.'

When I got off the bus, I thought I was too early, because at first I didn't see Rachel. Then I looked again at a girl sitting on a bench. She didn't have the long blonde hair that had always made Rachel stand out in a crowd. Instead, she had a short crop-cut, like someone out of a prison camp.

'Rachel! You've had your hair cut!' I tried to sound admiring rather than dismayed.

Don't get me wrong... she was still beautiful. No haircut could change her face, which was as perfect as a Beauty Queen Barbie doll's. Or her slim figure, or her confidence in herself. (Anyone who's confident is halfway to being attractive, no matter what they look like.)

'Do you like it? I thought it would look more grown-up. I'm tired of being treated like a little kid. Plus it annoyed my mum.' She smiled maliciously, and I saw she hadn't changed much. Still the same Rachel.

She wanted to know why I needed to buy clothes Mum wouldn't like. I told her about the party.

'I haven't been to a party in ages,' she said, looking wistful. 'Why didn't Debs invite me? I've known her for years.'

'She didn't give out invites, she just told everyone at The Garret. If you'd been there, you would have been included. But you've sort of disappeared from view. It's almost like you died.'

'So you don't think she'd mind if I turned up? I could tell Mum and Dad that Debs is a new friend from Highfield. They'd like that. They might let me go to the party.'

'Oh, they do let you out occasionally, then?'

'Yes – if I've been a good little girl and done all my homework.' She scowled. 'They are being so horrible to me. And the worst thing is, they keep telling me it's all for my own good. They want me to pass loads of exams and go to uni and get boring jobs like they've got. But that isn't what I want to do with my life!'

'What *do* you want to do with your life?' I asked.

'Be famous. Have a good time and make lots of money. I dunno… get on TV somehow, become a celebrity… You don't do that by getting ten GCSEs.'

I wondered what she thought she might get to be famous for. She had her looks, of course, but she was far too small to be a model, and she couldn't sing or dance, or do anything much except look good. (Of course, you could say the same about lots of famous people.)

We headed towards the shops. I had brought all my babysitting money with me – saving up for new glasses could wait for a week or two – but I soon saw it wasn't going to go very far. Not in the expensive shops that Rachel liked.

After trying on lots of things I couldn't afford, I suggested looking around the market. This was better. I bought two tops and a short black skirt. The only problem was, I couldn't try them on.

'We could go into a shop, and use their changing room,' Rachel suggested.

In a big shop she selected a pair of jeans, and we found a changing room. I was pleased with my new clothes. (Definitely the sort of thing that Mum would hate.) The tight green top looked quite sexy, and I knew my legs were good enough for the skirt. Shoes, though... I needed some shoes with more of a heel.

Meanwhile Rachel was admiring herself in the jeans.

'Are you going to get them?' I asked.

'I can't. Like I said, my parents are really mean about money these days.'

Looking depressed, she handed the jeans back to the girl on duty, who hung them on a rail by the changing-room door. We went out. But before we'd gone very far, Rachel stopped suddenly.

'My phone! I must have left it in the changing room. Wait here.'

She went back into the shop. A minute later I heard an alarm go off – the kind of alarm that shops have in their doorways to trap shoplifters. Uh-oh...

Rachel came racing out of the shop, dodged past me and ran down a side street. She had disappeared before the shop security guard reached the door. I saw him look upwards at the security camera. Rachel might have been caught on camera as she dashed out. And what about earlier? Would I be on camera too, walking around the shop with a thief?

As casually as I could, I strolled off down the street. No one followed me. But I couldn't get rid of the anxious feeling crawling around inside my stomach.

A few minutes later, Rachel texted me. We met up at a pizza place on the corner. She was grinning all over her face.

'You got the jeans, then,' I said.

'Yeah,' she said, patting her shoulder bag. 'But I can't get the security tag off. I'd better not go into any more shops. I'll set all the alarms going.'

'You do realise you're probably on security camera?'

'So? All they'll have is my picture, not my name, address and phone number. Don't look so worried, Emma. I just have to remember not to go into that shop for a few weeks.'

She never worries. That's one of her problems. A bit of worry is quite healthy – it stops you doing crazy things without thinking.

'What's the matter?' she asked. 'It's been a good morning. You got the things you need, and so did I.'

'Like you really need some jeans you can't wear anywhere near a shop doorway.'

'I didn't mean that. A bit of excitement is what I meant. You can't imagine how boring my life is at the moment.' She looked at her watch. 'Oh, help... got to go. We must do this again sometime. I'll call you, okay?'

6

Party time

It was Saturday. Party day.

The problem of getting changed without Mum seeing me was easily solved – I went round to Charlie's to get ready. Charlie's mum had offered to give us a lift to the party. Mum had said firmly that she would pick me up at eleven o'clock.

'But Mum! The party's not finishing until midnight!'

'Well, in my opinion that's *far* too late for people your age.'

Nothing I could say would persuade her. She said, 'You ought to be thankful I'm letting you go to the party at all. And if you keep on making such a fuss, I might change my mind.'

Getting changed at Charlie's, I found myself wishing my mum was more like hers. Charlie's mum must be 20 years younger than mine, and she's interested in clothes and make-up and stuff. She let me borrow a pair of her shoes. They were so high-heeled that I could hardly walk in them, but they made my legs look terrific.

We had taken so long getting ready that when we got there, the party was in full swing. Debs let us in, and I enjoyed the look of shock on her face at the sight of my short skirt. (She usually saw me on a Sunday in my Eunice clothes.)

And I certainly got more attention than usual from the boys. I heard Harry say, 'Who's that?'

Joe muttered, 'It's what's-her-name, Una... Eunice... You know, her dad's the vicar.'

'You're having a laugh,' said Harry, staring at me. 'Must be her long-lost non-identical twin.'

'Nice legs, shame about the face,' said Joe. As I walked past him, I managed to stab his foot with my high-heeled shoe – he yelped in agony.

'Nice face, shame about the foot,' I said. 'Actually, I lied about the face.'

Abena was already there – she only lived around the corner. So was Kwami, her older brother, and a friend of his, a guy I'd never seen before. I liked the look of him. He was tall and broad-shouldered, with a brilliant smile.

Knowing that I looked good made me more confident than usual. When Kwami's friend smiled at me, I smiled back, and waited for him to come and talk to me.

It was some time before he made a move. Meanwhile, I danced with my friends and had a few drinks – non-alcoholic, of course. Debs' mum was around, keeping an eye on things. (I wondered if she knew about the group of boys at the bottom of the garden. They were probably drinking something stronger than lemonade.)

Then Kwami's friend came up to us. He pretended it was Abena he wanted to speak to, but all the time he was looking at me.

'What is your name?' he asked me. 'I am Yao.'

Unlike Abena and Kwami, who had lived in Birton since they were young, he sounded very African. His voice was deep. If he was in the same year as Kwami, he must be about 16.

I really hoped Rachel would walk in at that moment, and find me talking to the best-looking guy at the party. Rachel had a built-in satnav system to track down fit guys. No… on second thoughts, it might be better if she didn't appear.

Abena, tired of being ignored, went away, leaving the two of us in a corner. Because of the loud music, we had to stand close together to hear what was said. (Well, that's my excuse, anyway.) He leaned against the wall, looking down at me. He had the most amazing deep brown eyes.

When I asked him about his home country, his smile faded away. He told me about the war which was tearing the country apart. Two of his cousins had been killed, and his whole family had been in danger, because they belonged to the side which was losing the war. That was why they had come to England.

'We are lucky. We had some money, so we could get out. I do not know if we will ever go back. It's very dangerous.'

'Do you want to go back?' I asked him.

'Yes. Oh, yes.' His face was full of longing. 'This is a good place to live, but it is not my home.'

I'd never met anyone before who had lived through a war (apart from Great Uncle Maurice, aged 80, and not nearly as good-looking as Yao). I was quite impressed. We talked for ages.

But then Joe had to come along.

'You think you're in with a chance?' he said to Yao. 'You're wasting your time, mate.'

He had definitely been drinking. I could tell by the smell of his breath.

'Just ignore him,' I said to Yao. 'He might go away.'

Joe said, 'She's a good little girl. Her dad's a vicar. She's as frigid as a… as a fridge.'

I was annoyed now. 'Joe, I've got news for you. Just because a girl doesn't fancy you, it doesn't mean she has to be frigid. Maybe she just doesn't like you much. Could that be possible?'

Joe shook his head. 'They all like me. All the girls.'

'Not half as much as you like yourself,' I muttered.

'What did you say?'

'I said, not half as much as you like yourself.'

That annoyed him, I could tell. He struggled to find an answer, but the drink was obviously fuddling his brain. 'Same to you,' was all he could come up with.

'It's getting a bit crowded in here,' I said to Yao. 'And hot. Let's go outside for a bit.'

I wasn't lying. It *was* hot, and I was starting to get a headache – probably because I wasn't wearing my glasses, but no way was I going to put them on now, and ruin my image.

Outside, it was dark, and the air was cool. The garden smelt dewy and fresh. It could have been so romantic, if it weren't for the starless, orange glow of the city sky, and the roar of traffic.

We walked down the garden. I could feel my heels sinking into the lawn, making me lurch drunkenly, but Yao held my arm.

The boys had disappeared from the bottom of the garden – they must have run out of drink. There was no one around. Yao led me to the side of the shed, under a tree. Something rustled in the undergrowth, and I could smell compost from the bin, but I didn't care. I knew he was going to kiss me.

I had never kissed a boy before. At the thought, excitement leapt through me, sharp and prickly as static. What would it be like? Would I make a fool of myself?

He held me in his arms. His kiss was gentle at first, as if he expected me to leap away. Then, when I kissed him back, he gave a sigh and started kissing me as if he meant it… as if we were deeply in love and about to be parted for ever.

At last we stopped for breath.

'You are very nice,' he whispered. 'What is your name?'

'Emma,' I reminded him – feeling rather hurt that he'd forgotten.

'Emma,' he murmured. 'Yes.'

He was kissing me again. Then I felt his hand start to slide up underneath my top.

Hey, wait a minute, I wanted to say. *We've only just met!* But I didn't want him to think that Joe had been right about me, so I kept quiet.

Suddenly I heard the mutter of voices in the darkness.

'Over there. Snogging by the shed.'

'Where? I don't believe you.'

'There, see? Are you blind?'

It was Joe and Harry. I stepped away from Yao as if he was suddenly burning hot.

'What pathetic lives you must lead,' I said angrily, 'if you have to get your kicks from spying on other people.'

'Pathetic... yeah, someone's going to look pathetic all right,' said Joe, grinning. 'Someone's mummy has come looking for her. We'd better tell her to try the garden.'

'What? Oh help – I have to go,' I told Yao, and hurried towards the house.

Trust Mum to spoil everything... But secretly I couldn't help feeling a tiny bit relieved.

7

Real and unreal

Mum was standing in the hall, trying to make polite conversation with Debs' mum above the noise of the party. When she saw me, her eyes widened. Of course, I was still wearing my party clothes and borrowed shoes. Mum must have come early – I meant to give myself time to change before she arrived.

She didn't say anything, naturally. Not in front of Debs' mum. But she gave me a look that meant, *The party's over*. I knew exactly how Cinderella must have felt as the clock struck midnight. Back to the cinders and rags... and it was only ten to eleven. So unfair!

As soon as we were in the car, Mum started in on me. 'Where did you get those dreadful clothes? And the shoes?' she demanded.

'I borrowed them. Don't you like them?'

'Don't try to play Miss Innocent with me! You know what I've always taught you about how to dress, yet you look like a...' She couldn't bring herself to say the word she really meant. 'Like a street-walker. What will people think? They'll say the vicar can't keep his own daughter in order.'

'But Mum, this is what people wear to parties nowadays. Things have changed since you were young. Didn't you see the other girls tonight, and what they were wearing?'

'Yes, I saw them.' Her voice was stiff with disapproval. 'What are their mothers thinking of?'

Mum has what it takes to be a great prime minister. She's always so sure she's in the right and everyone else is wrong.

'Know who lent me these shoes?' I said. 'Charlie's mum.'

Mum didn't believe me. 'Even if Charlie's mother possessed a pair of shoes like that, I hope she would have more sense than—'

'Charlie's mum doesn't dress like an old lady, and she doesn't make Charlie dress like one either. 'Specially not for a party. I just *can't* go to parties in the sort of clothes you've always bought for me.'

'Oh, can't you?' she snapped. 'In that case the answer's simple. You won't go to any more parties.'

'Mum! You can't say that! I'm nearly 14. You can't go on treating me like a 6-year-old for the rest of my life!'

'It's for your own good,' she said coldly, starting the engine.

By now I was furious. 'That's not true. It's for *your* own good,' I said. 'All you care about is what people think of you. *What will people think?* You say that all the time!'

'I don't see that you're any different,' said Mum. 'All you care about is what your silly little friends think. And if you don't look out, you'll end up just like them. Drinking. Taking drugs. Getting into trouble.'

This was ridiculous – completely over the top. 'Listen to yourself, Mum! Just because I got dressed up for a party, you think I'm about to ruin my whole life? I don't know how you can be so stupid.'

Abruptly she stopped the car. 'That's not the way to talk to your mother!'

I didn't answer.

'I will not have you behaving like this! Apologise, or you can get out of the car right now and walk home!'

I almost did that, just to show her. I didn't believe she would really let me walk home alone late at night. What stopped me was the thought of walking any further in those crippling shoes. I already felt as if my toes had been squeezed to death.

'I'm waiting,' Mum said icily. 'An apology, please.'

'Sorry,' I muttered.

She could probably tell by my voice that I didn't mean it. But she let it pass. We drove on again in grim silence.

For about the thousandth time, I wished I had a different mother. Mum was so fixed in her ways. Old-fashioned. Just plain old – more like a granny than a mother.

I had a sudden weird thought. Perhaps I had stumbled on something. Could it be that – like Tia in *Southside*, my favourite soap – I had been brought up by my grandparents, all the time believing they were my mum and dad? Or could I have been adopted?

If Mum and Dad weren't my real parents, it would explain a lot. Their age… their outdated ideas… the way I sometimes felt I didn't love them... all this would be natural if my real parents were somewhere else. Completely different people, more like me.

Perhaps my real mum had me when she was very young. She couldn't give me a proper home, so she put me up for adoption. Mum and Dad had chosen me, and they loved me so much, they never managed to tell me that I wasn't really their child.

The thought made me feel quite strange. If everything I knew about myself was based on a lie, then how could I be certain of anything at all? Real/unreal, true/false... all mixed up, shuffled like cards and dealt out, flipped over, shuffled again...

'Well? Are you planning to sit there all night?'

Mum's voice broke into my thoughts. The car had stopped, and I hadn't even noticed. I got out slowly, still thinking.

Dad opened the door to us. (He hadn't come to fetch me because his Saturday night was always given over to preparing for Sunday.) He didn't seem to notice me looking at him oddly. He didn't notice what I was wearing, either. No doubt Mum would mention it soon enough.

'Was it a good party?' he asked me.

'Pretty good.' Obviously I couldn't tell him why. 'There were lots of people there from the youth group – we had a great time.'

He smiled. 'I'm so glad you're finding friends of your own age.'

Friends... maybe even a boyfriend. I realised I hadn't had time to give Yao my number. But if he wanted to see me again, he could always send a message by way of Kwami and Abena.

You are very nice, he had said. So I must have done all right at the kissing game. But I wasn't sure I wanted to go out with him. He was three years older than me, and he'd probably had loads of girlfriends. He had seemed pretty keen on trying to take things further than kissing. How far would he expect me to go? The thought scared me. I didn't want to end up like Simone, a girl in Year 10 who had to leave school because she had a baby.

Naturally, I told Charlie and Abena what had happened at the party. (They already knew most of it, thanks to Joe and his big mouth.) I could see a flicker of envy on Charlie's face. I was pretty sure she'd never kissed a boy – I had raced ahead of her in the snakes-and-ladders game of dating.

I asked Abena what she knew about Yao. She told me where he lived, on the same estate as her own family, and which school he went to. Then she hesitated.

'Emma, don't get your hopes up too high. He's already got a girlfriend.'

'Has he?' I tried to sound casual, although I felt as if someone had punched me. 'So why didn't he take her to the party?'

'She was ill, Kwami says – otherwise she would have been there. So Yao was two-timing her.'

'Sounds like a really nice guy,' Charlie said sarcastically. But I knew she was only jealous. She would have swapped places with me any day.

Abena looked at me anxiously, to see if I had been hurt by the news. I pretended not to care. Snakes and ladders… up a ladder, down a snake… it was what you had to expect.

'Not that I'm breaking my heart over him,' I said, 'but why didn't you tell me he had a girlfriend?'

'I didn't know. Kwami told me later.'

'Anyway, my mum already ruined things,' I said. 'I mean, coming to collect me at ten to eleven! I suppose I was lucky she didn't get as far as the garden.'

****

I hadn't told anyone my thoughts about being adopted. But my mind kept returning to the idea. I couldn't leave it alone – like picking at a scab.

If you're adopted, I remembered reading somewhere, you can try to trace your real mother. But not until you reach the age of 18, which would mean another four years to wait. And even then, if your mother doesn't want to be found, you may get nowhere.

I could always ask my parents outright. 'Am I really your child, or did you adopt me?'

Dad, I was certain, would give me a straight answer, but the question would hurt him deeply. And I didn't want to hurt him. He wasn't the one I usually felt angry with.

Mum – if she had been lying to me all this time – would probably continue to lie. She always *said* that Christians should be honest, but sometimes she didn't quite live up to this. She would be shocked and horrified that I could even ask the question.

If I couldn't ask them, how could I find out?

I must have a birth certificate somewhere. It was probably locked in a drawer of Dad's desk, along with the other legal stuff – passports and wills and things. Maybe I could ask to see it. If they didn't want to show it to me, I would know there must be a reason…

One way or another, I was determined to find out the truth.

8

The locked drawer

I texted Rachel to ask her why she hadn't come to Debs' party, but she didn't answer. Then, a few days later, she rang me.

'I have to be quick,' she said. 'I'm totally out of credit, so I'm using the house phone, but Greta could come in at any minute. How about meeting up again, same time, same place?'

'Okay, but no more shoplifting,' I said. 'It makes me nervous.'

She laughed. 'We'll find something else to do, then.'

Bunking off school was just as easy as before. I met Rachel in town, and we went to a café.

'You'll have to pay, though,' Rachel said.

I wasn't used to Rachel being poverty-stricken. She always used to be the one with money. 'What's the matter?' I asked her. 'Have they stopped giving you pocket money?'

'It's not called pocket money now, I have to *earn* it. You know – by doing my homework and being a good little girl. This week I didn't get anything at all,' she said gloomily. 'Because Greta caught me trying to sneak out to the party.'

'Oh, so that's why you never turned up. What happened?'

'I said I was having an early night, and she seemed to believe me. After a while I got dressed and started climbing out of the window—'

'You climbed out of your window? Three floors up?' Sometimes I think she really is crazy.

'I thought I could get down the drainpipe onto the garage roof. It doesn't look all that far – I mean, even if I fell, I wouldn't kill myself, would I? But anyway, Greta must have heard something. I bet she was listening outside my door – the old cow! She came barging in, and pulled me back inside the window, and then she locked it and took away the key. So now I can't even open my own window. Honestly, it's like being in prison.'

'That sounds pretty bad,' I said. 'Have you told your parents how horrible she is?'

'I keep on telling them. But they won't listen. They think she's wonderful, and even my sister doesn't mind her too much. I hate her!'

I could see it was hard for Rachel having to live under a new, strict set of rules. Her parents used to be just the opposite – so busy with work that they let Rachel do whatever she wanted.

Rachel started plotting ways to get rid of Greta. Putting poison in her coffee seemed to be the favourite. Either that, or cutting the brakes on her car.

'You've been watching too much TV,' I told her.

'Well, what else is there to do? I hardly ever go out these days... But you haven't told me about the party.'

So I told her about meeting Yao. She wanted to know all the details.

'Did you like him a lot?'

'Well, yes, until he started trying to... you know... feel me up.'

'If you didn't want him to, why didn't you stop him?' Rachel demanded.

'I dunno. Because I wanted to make him like me, I suppose.'

She said, 'That's really dumb. Listen, boys will try to get off with you if you let them, but it doesn't mean they like you. Then they'll boast about it to their mates afterwards, and say what a slag you are. It's up to you to stop things going too far.'

'Yes, but how?'

She gave me a pitying look. 'Just say no. And if he won't listen, get rid of him. Boys are like buses – there'll be another one arriving soon.'

That was easy for her to say. There would always be boys waiting to ask Rachel out. But for me, the next bus might not appear for months.

'Hey, what's that?' Rachel said suddenly. She pointed to a boarded-up shop across the road. The front was covered with posters, including a large fluorescent orange one.

*** *STARMAKERS* ***

Auditions for the new series
Solo singers, groups and dancers needed
(minimum age 16)
Come to Birton Town Hall, 12 October, 10am

'*Starmakers*,' she breathed. 'I'd love to be on that.'
'You're not 16,' I reminded her.
'I can make myself look 16 – easy.'
'And don't you have to be able to sing or dance?'

'Oh, anyone can sing. And I did go to dance classes for a while. This could be my big chance, Emma! My chance to be famous!' She counted off the days. 'The 12th of October – that's next week. I'd have to bunk off school again, but it would be worth it. Want to come?'

'Maybe,' I said cautiously. I quite liked the idea of seeing what went on at the *Starmakers* auditions. 'But what if we get filmed, and someone sees us?'

'That's the whole point, you idiot. I get filmed and millions of people see me. And the boss of Max Factor or L'Oréal sees me and says, "There – that one. Find her! That's the new face we want to launch our new lipstick," or whatever.'

Yeah, in your dreams, Rachel.

I said, 'I didn't mean that. I meant, what if someone like a teacher sees us? Or my mum?'

'Your mum watches *Starmakers* a lot, does she?'

'No, she can't stand it.'

'Well then. What are you worried about?'

In the end I decided to go along with her, although nothing would persuade me to take part in the actual audition. I would simply be there to keep Rachel company, and give her a shoulder to cry on when she got rejected.

As for missing a whole day of school, I didn't care about that. Probably no one would notice. Anyway, schoolwork had slid a long way down my list of priorities.

****

I'd been waiting for the chance to find out some more about my family background. It came one evening when Dad was out.

The nights were getting chilly. Mum lit the gas fire in the living room, and as she sat down, she sighed.

'What's the matter?' I asked her.

'I was just thinking, this fire's a lot less work than the log fires we had at home... I mean, in Nembury. But it doesn't look as nice.'

'No,' I said, remembering how the living flames used to dance and leap. And how the rug used to smoulder, when sparks jumped out. And how, if you forgot to put more logs on, the fire quickly died down to grey ashes. (Sometimes the old ways aren't so great after all – but try telling Mum that.)

Was she still missing the old life? I wasn't. The crumbling vicarage... the huge, untidy garden... the sleepy village, where there was nothing at all for young people to do... But then, Mum wasn't young any more. She'd never understood how bored I had been in Nembury.

'Mum,' I said, 'do you have any photos of you when you were my age? Can I see?'

She dug out an old, fading album. There were photos of her and her brother, mostly taken on holiday in places like Blackpool. She had long hair then, pulled back into a ponytail, which didn't really suit her solemn, square face. The biggest shock was the shortness of her skirts.

'Mum! Did you really wear skirts like that?'

'Everyone did,' she said defensively. 'It was the Sixties.'

'So how can you complain about what I was wearing to the party the other day?'

She looked taken aback. Then she laughed. (It's a pity she doesn't laugh more – it makes her look so much younger.)

'All right, point taken,' she said.

I looked at my own face in the mirror above the fireplace, holding up the album beside it.

'We don't look all that much alike, do we?' I said as casually as I could. 'You and me, I mean.'

'No. You take after your father's side of the family. Look…'

She took out another album, an even older one, and flicked through it. 'Your grandmother, Dad's mother… you won't remember her, she died when you were a baby. But you do look rather like her when she was young.'

She showed me a fading, grey photo. From under an old-fashioned felt hat, my own face stared out at me. Apart from having a bigger chin, Dad's mother looked exactly like me.

This wasn't what I had been expecting – not at all. It seemed to prove that I couldn't be adopted. I really was Dad's child, and I had inherited his mother's face (though not her chin, fortunately).

So my theory was wrong. Was that good or bad? I wasn't sure.

It wasn't until later, lying in bed, that I thought of something else. The photos didn't prove anything about my blood relationship to Mum. Dad could be my real father, even though Mum wasn't my real mother. He could have been married before. Mum could be my stepmother.

No, that was silly. They would have told me. Why would they keep it a secret? I mean, there's nothing shameful about being married twice, or being a stepmother (except in fairy tales, where stepmothers are always mean, rotten and nasty).

It all came back to my birth certificate. Although I'd never seen it, I had a vague idea that it would name both my parents, and say when they were married.

Next day, I asked Mum if I could look at my birth certificate because we were talking about them at school. She gave me an odd kind of look, but went off to Dad's study. My guess had been right – I heard her unlocking his desk.

The certificate was a single sheet of paper giving my date and place of birth; my name (Eunice Emma Todd, female); Dad's name (Giles Henry Todd, Clerk in Holy Orders); and Mum's name (Marjorie Susan Todd, maiden surname Bowyer).

'What's a maiden surname?' I asked Mum.

'It means the name I was born with. I was Marjorie Bowyer before I married your father.'

'And when was that?'

'Eighteen years before you were born,' said Mum.

Of course, I knew that. It was all part of the story I had grown up with. Mum and Dad, childless for years, longing for a baby... then suddenly I arrived, like a miracle. An answer to prayer.

Now that I thought about it, wasn't there something odd about that story? It was quite rare, surely, to have a baby after all those years of trying, unless there was some kind of medical help. I had vaguely heard of a process where doctors could give a woman an egg donated by someone else. Inside her body it would grow into a baby... 'her' child, although it wouldn't look like her. It would look like the real mother, who had donated the egg.

That was possible. Or maybe Mum, desperate for a child, had stolen me out of a pram? My thoughts were getting wilder and wilder.

Mum went to put my birth certificate back in the desk, and I followed her. Just then, the study phone rang.

While she was answering it ('No, I'm terribly sorry, he's out visiting... can I be of any help?') I had a look in the desk drawer. There were other certificates in there, folded up. I took one out and unfolded it. I saw it was Mum and Dad's marriage certificate – but that was all I had time to notice. Because Mum, still talking away, had snatched it out of my hand.

'Mum! I was looking at that,' I protested.

She ignored me. 'Well, thank you so much for volunteering to help. Giles will be really grateful, I know... Yes, of course. Goodbye.'

'Can't I see it?' I said, as she folded up the paper.

'No.' She put it away, closed the drawer and locked it. 'It's nothing to do with you.'

'I don't understand. What's the problem? I only want to have a look...'

'Eunice, no means no.' And she slid the key into her apron pocket. Then she went out, leaving me staring at the locked drawer.

Weird… really weird. What could be so secret about a marriage certificate? She had made me extremely curious.

Naturally I looked for the key over the next few days. I looked in all her usual hiding places, and a lot more places I'd never tried before. But I couldn't find it.

9

Rules 'n' regulations

On Sunday, Mark was in charge at The Garret. He started things off by getting everyone to play a new game involving three teams, a tennis ball, a cricket bat, and a large chalk circle on the floor of the hall. The trouble was, he didn't explain the rules very well.

'Rules?' he said, looking vague. 'Oh, don't worry. Make it up as you go along. Have fun!' And he wandered off towards the kitchen.

The result was chaos. Some of the older boys started enforcing their idea of how the game should be played. The younger boys argued with them – they just wanted to play football. Most of the girls dropped out altogether. Then Harry threw down the bat in disgust, and hit Alex on the foot.

'Okay, stop,' Mark shouted. 'What went wrong?'

'We didn't know how to play,' said Joe. 'You never explained the rules properly.'

'But there aren't any rules.' Mark sounded surprised. 'Rules are just a nuisance. Why should you have to do what other people tell you? It's better if everyone makes their own decisions… isn't it?'

'No! You can't have a game without rules,' various people tried to tell him. 'It's just stupid.'

'Actually, I agree with you,' said Mark. Then he sat us down and started his talk, which was all about – surprise, surprise – the need for having rules. He talked about the Ten Commandments that God gave to Moses, and we tried to remember what they were.

'Don't kill. Don't steal.'

'Don't sleep around.'

'Respect your father and mother.'

'Don't lie about other people.'

'That's five,' said Mark. 'Not bad. Can anyone remember the other five?'

'Er… don't fight? Is that one?'

'It can't be. There are loads of wars in the Bible.'

'Don't get found out?'

I knew the whole lot, but I kept my mouth shut. I didn't want to look like a know-all. In the end we looked them up in the Bible (Exodus chapter 20).

'People have forgotten these rules,' said Mark. 'And that's why the world is getting more chaotic every day.'

He handed out some newspapers, asking us to look for headlines which involved God's commandments being broken. They were on almost every page:

GIRL OF 17 STABBED BY MUGGER

CHILD RAPIST ON TRIAL

STOLEN BANK DETAILS ON SALE FOR £5

MP LIED IN COURT

'None of this would happen if people obeyed God's rules,' he said. Then he asked us all to think about what we had done in the last few days. How many of the Ten Commandments had we managed to obey?

'Well, I definitely haven't murdered anyone,' said Harry.

Joe said, 'Me neither. And I haven't coveted anyone's cattle or donkeys.'

'Anyone manage ten out of ten?' asked Mark, but no one said they had. Although I knew all the commandments, I certainly hadn't kept them all. *Respect your father and mother* – that was a tough one. And then there was the very first command: *I am the Lord your God… do not worship any god except me.*

If God really existed, that was surely the most important command of all. If he didn't, then it was meaningless.

'When people forget about worshipping God,' said Mark, 'what do they worship?'

'Nothing,' said Charlie.

'That's where you're wrong. People love and worship all kinds of things. They love money, or fame or looks. Or maybe they love a person. If your boyfriend or girlfriend is the most important thing in your life – if you would do absolutely anything for them – it's like they are taking the place of God in your life.'

When he mentioned fame, I thought of Rachel. She was desperate to be famous. She'd be quite happy to break every rule in the book, if it would bring her fame. So, yes… you could say that was her main aim in life. Her purpose – her god.

And what about me? Hmmm… The thing I had always wanted was to be popular. To be at the centre of the crowd. To have girls like me and boys fancy me – that was why I'd reinvented myself and changed from Eunice to Emma.

Mark said, 'God created us to be his children. He wants us to love him as a father. If we ignore him, there will always be a God-shaped gap at the inner heart of our lives. We can try to fill the gap with other things that we think will make us happy. But that doesn't work, not for long.'

It *is* working, I wanted to say to him. I'm happier now than I used to be when I was trying to keep all the rules.

Rules are just a nuisance. Who needs them? Simply make it up as you go along. And don't worry… be happy.

****

'Has anyone booked a sitter for the weekend?' asked Charlie.

I shook my head. It was like that sometimes – a whole weekend when no one needed us.

'It's only Monday,' said Abena. 'They could still ring before Friday.'

'I hope they do,' I said. 'I'm skint again.' Although I was trying to save up for my new glasses, I kept thinking of other things I needed money for. My savings were growing about as quickly as moss grows on a stone.

'You know what? We ought to advertise more,' said Charlie. 'At the moment we're only getting customers from church. If we put an advert somewhere else, like in a shop window…'

So, on the way home, we stopped to look at the ads in a newsagent's window.

'I wonder how much it costs to advertise?' said Charlie.

'Only 50p a week. It says so, there,' I pointed out.

'Why don't we try advertising for a week?' Abena suggested. 'If we start getting bookings from it, we could leave the ad there all the time.'

We went into the shop, asked for a card, and put our advert together. At the back of my mind was a slight niggle of unease, because my mum wouldn't approve of this. She had agreed to the babysitting idea, as long as we only advertised in the church newsletter.

But she would never know. She wasn't likely to see this ad, in a small, back-street shop near school. If we got any bookings from it, I could tell Mum that one of our regulars had recommended us to a friend. It would be fine. Don't worry…

As Charlie paid for the ad, I glanced at the local papers on display. A headline caught my eye. There was something on the front page that Dad ought to see.

BIRTON RESIDENTS OPPOSE CHURCH PLANS

Local residents have objected to plans for a drop-in centre for homeless people at St Jude's church hall.

They handed in a petition signed by 142 people, all opposed to the scheme, to the council offices on Friday.

'We don't have anything against homeless people,' said Josephine Grant (57), leader of the residents' group. 'We simply don't think Church Street is the right kind of area for a plan like this.'

I bought the paper to show Dad that Mum had been right – the neighbours wouldn't like his idea. And that would worry Mum, because she hated upsetting anyone.

There was a bit of an atmosphere at home these days. Whenever Dad mentioned the homeless project, Mum went rather quiet. But Dad didn't seem to notice – he was too caught up in his plans. He appeared to have forgotten the incident when the stranger came to our door. I was pretty sure Mum hadn't forgotten, though. A sort of shiver went through her sometimes, when the doorbell rang at night.

'Oh, how typical,' said Charlie, reading over my shoulder. 'My mum says Church Street's full of NIMBYs.'

'NIMBYs? What are they?' asked Abena.

'Not In My Back Yard, it means. People who say, oh yes, go ahead with your plans, but not here. Not near my house, in my nice, peaceful street.'

'Selfish people, in other words,' said Abena.

'Selfish, or sensible?' I asked. 'I mean, who wants a load of druggies and drunks wandering past their home every day? The crime rate will probably go up too.'

The others laughed, as if they thought I was being sarcastic.

'What's funny?' I said, annoyed. 'I'm serious. Oh, it's all right for you two – you don't live in Church Street.'

Then I told myself not to worry. Dad's plan might never get off the ground, if the neighbours had their way. Anyway, I had more interesting things to think about… like the *Starmakers* auditions tomorrow.

Did Rachel have *Starmakers* quality? I didn't think so – but it would be fun finding out.

10

Last Minute

The auditions were supposed to start at 10. We were late, because there was no way of avoiding the school run without giving away our secret. At the bus station, Rachel got changed into a clingy black dress, with a tight belt to show off her tiny waist. By the time she had done her make-up, she looked about 18.

'Nervous?' I asked her.

'Of course I'm nervous,' she said irritably. 'Wouldn't you be?'

'You don't look it,' I assured her. 'You look great.'

When we arrived at the Town Hall, we found an enormous queue, zigzagging between barriers, almost filling Market Square. It was moving forwards very slowly. Clearly, it didn't matter that we were late, because it would be hours before we reached the front door.

'Some people have been here since 5am,' said the woman in front of us. She was quite chatty. Her name was Lauren. She was in her twenties, small, round-faced and plain-looking, the sort of person you hardly notice when you pass them in the street. She was a hairdresser, she told us, but she'd always wanted to sing.

'What song are you going to perform?' she asked Rachel. 'I'm going to do "Summertime".' She sang us the first verse, and she had a lovely voice – not that anyone noticed. Plenty of other people were warming up their voices, or doing stretching exercises right there in the queue, with intense concentration on their faces.

When Rachel tried out her chosen song, Lauren listened carefully. Then she said, 'Are you sure that's the right song for you? It's quite hard to sing.' (A polite way of saying: That was terrible.)

Rachel tried a different song, but I could tell she wasn't singing in tune. 'Maybe the first one was better,' I said.

'Oh, do you think so? I can't decide,' she said.

I didn't think either song would get her very far. Her voice was just a pale shadow of Lauren's. But of course, looks were important too. The *Starmakers* judges wouldn't select anyone with an 'image problem' – meaning ugly or fat or odd-looking people. Their ideal contestant would have Rachel's face and Lauren's effortless, soaring voice.

It was starting to rain, and we hadn't brought an umbrella. Lauren let us share hers, which was nice of her. Three people under one umbrella meant that none of us stayed very dry. But nothing could discourage Rachel.

Slowly we shuffled forwards. By lunchtime we had covered about half the distance across the square.

'You're going to miss your afternoon registration at school,' I warned Rachel.

'I don't care. This is more important.'

I was getting hungry – unlike Rachel, who was too nervous to eat – so I ducked out of the queue and ran to a sandwich bar across the square. As I returned, I caught the tail end of an announcement.

'... and thank you for coming. The next *Starmakers* auditions will be in Manchester on 15 October.'

Rachel and Lauren were looking upset. 'They say they've found enough solo singers,' said Rachel angrily. 'They told us to go home.'

'Well, that was a waste of time,' I said. 'We didn't even get inside the doors.'

'Wait a minute.' Rachel grabbed my arm. 'They're still looking for dancers and groups. We might get in if we go as a group – all three of us. Lauren, are you up for it?'

'Are you crazy?' I said. 'We've never even sung together.'

But Lauren seemed interested. 'It might be worth a try. Anything's better than just going home without being seen.'

'Oh, no,' I said panicking. 'I can't sing. And I'm not dressed for this. I'll look a total idiot.'

'You look OK,' said Rachel. 'You can borrow some of my make-up. Oh go on, Emma, please. Say you'll do it. This is my big chance!'

'And mine,' said Lauren. 'I mean, what's the worst that can happen?'

'Getting savaged by the judges,' I said. 'I can just imagine what they'll say about us.'

'Look, most likely we won't even meet the judges,' Lauren said. 'They don't see everybody – they don't have time. Only a few people get selected to meet them. I know because my cousin went to the London auditions. She never got to see the judges, and she was so disappointed. She loves Tony Stewart.'

In the end, the two of them managed to persuade me. By now, a large section of the queue had melted away, and we had almost reached the doors of the Town Hall.

'We need a song,' said Rachel. 'What about that one you were singing, Lauren? Teach it to us.'

We tried to sing it together. But Lauren stopped halfway through.

'Look, don't worry about trying to do harmonies,' she said to Rachel. 'It's too complicated and we don't have time to practise. Just sing the tune.'

'I *was* singing the tune. Wasn't I?'

Lauren sighed. 'Let's try it again.'

This time it sounded slightly better. Not great, but better.

'What are we calling ourselves?' I asked. 'If we're a group, we have to have a name.'

'The Umbrella Girls,' suggested Lauren.

'Mmm... sounds a bit naff, don't you think?'

'Q3,' said Rachel. 'Because we met in a queue.'

We argued for a while. We were coming up to the desk where names were being taken and numbers given out, and still we couldn't agree.

'How about Last Minute?' I said. So that became our name.

Inside the entrance hall, there was more queuing. Someone came down the line, asking for dancers and directing them to the basement. That left only the groups.

In front of us was what Lauren called a 'barbershop quartet' – four men who sounded as if they'd sung together for the last 30 years. In fact, that was the main thing against them – their age. Behind us were three girls who looked like sisters, wearing identical outfits. Again, being sisters, they had probably sung together before. Unlike us.

'Should we have one more practice?' Lauren suggested.

We went through the song again. I knew it didn't sound right – the three sisters seemed to be trying not to giggle. But suddenly a cameraman homed in, and a face I knew appeared right next to us. It was Nicci Malone, the new *Starmakers* presenter! Practically standing on my feet!

'And who are you?' she said to Rachel. 'Tell us the name of your group.'

'Last Minute,' said Rachel, with a big smile directed at the camera. 'Because we haven't been together for very long.'

'What kind of music do you perform?'

'Oh, anything. Everything.'

'We're going to sing 'Summertime', said Lauren, but the cameraman ignored her. It was Rachel he wanted to film.

'And what do you do when you're not singing?' asked Nicci.

'Well, er… Lauren's a hairdresser. Emma and me, we're still at school, but of course we'll leave if *Starmakers* gives us our big break. Do you think we have a chance?'

Nicci said, 'Everyone has a chance on *Starmakers!* Good luck to Last Minute. We'll be back to see how they get on.'

She moved away, and the cameraman followed her.

'Wow!' said Rachel, looking dazed. 'I have actually spoken to Nicci Malone! I'd love to do her job. That would be my ideal career – presenter on *Starmakers*. I bet she makes loads of money, and she's famous.' She looked wistfully after Nicci. 'And she's really nice, too. Friendly.'

'Yeah, while the camera's on her,' said Lauren. 'I bet she's not so nice in real life. I read some things about her in the paper…' But there she stopped, because we were moving forward again.

The four guys in front of us were taken through a door. We couldn't hear what went on beyond it, but a short while later, they came out of a different door, looking depressed.

'They didn't get chosen,' I said. 'But they sounded really good!'

'Too old, I suppose,' said Lauren.

Then it was our turn to go through the door. It led, not to a stage, but to a small, square room. I saw that Lauren had been right. We weren't going to see the famous *Starmakers* judges – at least, not right now. It was two anonymous men who were about to decide our fate.

We sang the first verse of 'Summertime'. I thought it was our best effort so far. I held my breath. The two men looked at each other, and one of them nodded.

'Go on through into the holding area,' the other one told us. 'We'd like you to sing for the judges.'

As we went out, Rachel pinched my arm. 'See? I knew we could do it. We're on our way!'

'Yeah, and now we've got to sing for Tony Stewart,' I reminded her. 'Mr Nasty himself.'

The holding area was a large room with – guess what – another queue. Even though we'd got this far, there were loads of other groups waiting to see the judges. Some looked cool and confident, others seemed terrified.

'How did *they* get through?' muttered Lauren. She was looking at five boys who could easily have won an award for the World's Ugliest Boy Band. 'I heard them practising, earlier. They were terrible.'

'Well, they have to let a few hopeless ones through for the judges to be rude about,' I said. 'It makes good TV.'

Secretly, I was wondering if we came into that category. The hopeless cases – the tone-deaf ones – the people who should never in a million years be allowed to sing in public.

'Emma, we have to do something about your make-up and hair,' said Lauren.

Her hairdressing skills and Rachel's make-up made me look a bit more glamorous, but there wasn't much we could do about my clothes – plain school skirt and white shirt. I told myself it didn't matter. Nothing could really improve our chances, except a backing track to mime to, so that we didn't actually have to sing.

We waited and waited. At 3.30 I texted Charlie to tell her I wouldn't be walking home after school. She wanted to know where I was, but I didn't answer.

Meanwhile, Rachel was calling Greta, the housekeeper.

'What did you tell her?' I asked.

'The truth.'

'Was she mad at you?'

Rachel grinned. 'I knew it would be OK – she loves *Starmakers*. She made me promise to tell her all the backstage gossip. I'd better try and think of some.'

Slowly the room was emptying, as the different groups were called out one by one. At last it was our turn.

'Come on. We have to do this,' Rachel muttered fiercely. 'We have to get through to the next round.'

I didn't care about the next round. All I wanted was to survive the next few minutes without looking a complete idiot. I felt sick with nerves.

Then the door opened, and we stepped inside to face the judges.

11

Desperate

They sat at a table, facing us across an empty expanse of floor. They looked exactly as I'd seen them on TV – wise old Paul, kind Kate, and handsome, horrible Tony. On either side were cameras, aimed at us like missile launchers.

'Don't be frightened, girls. Come closer,' said Kate. 'Now, what are you going to sing for us?'

'Summertime', Lauren whispered, her voice shaking.

Three pairs of eyes were fixed on us. Three faces, one curious, one friendly and one critical, watched us to see what we could do. Were we *Starmakers* material?

The answer was no. Lauren, full of nerves, started off by singing too high. I could hear my voice going thin and squeaky, and Rachel's was in a different key altogether. We sounded absolutely awful. As we faltered to a stop, I could see that even Kate was struggling not to laugh out loud.

'What are you doing here, girls?' asked Tony. 'You're not a group. You're just three individuals attempting to sing the same song. At least, I *think* it was the same song. I'm not absolutely sure.'

'The girl on the left has a good voice,' said Paul. 'She would do better as a solo artiste. Come to the next auditions on your own, my dear, and you might have a chance.'

'It's a no from me as well, I'm afraid,' said Kate.

Feeling relieved – for they could have been a lot nastier – I turned to go. But Rachel wasn't ready to give up yet.

'Oh, please give us another chance,' she begged. 'I know we didn't sound too good, but we were nervous. We can do much better than that. Please!'

'Don't waste our time,' said Tony scornfully. 'Send in the next group!'

'No – wait a minute,' Rachel pleaded. 'I'm not doing this for me. It's for my mum. She's got cancer... they say she won't live until Christmas. It would mean so much to her to see me on TV. Please, please let us have another try.'

What an actress that girl would make! Her eyes had actually filled with tears. Instantly, she had Kate's sympathy, and Paul's as well. Only Tony looked impatient.

'Go on, then. We'll forget that first attempt,' said Paul. 'Start again.'

Rachel managed to put on a brave face, smiling through her tears. Lauren gripped her hand. We all took a deep breath...

This time, amazingly, everything went right. Even Rachel was singing in tune, and Lauren's strong voice held us all together.

'Well! That was much better,' said Kate. 'Your mum should be proud of you, love. I think you're very brave, and I'm going to vote yes.'

'It's still a no from me,' said Tony. 'We're judges, not counsellors. Are we going to vote for everyone who's ever suffered a tragedy in their life? Regardless of whether they can sing or not?'

Kate gave him a look of disgust. She said, 'Paul, you have the casting vote.'

Paul stared at each of us for a long, long moment, making his decision. Then he cleared his throat. 'I say yes. You're through to the next round.'

'Yes!' cried Rachel, hugging both of us. Then she turned to the judges. 'Oh, thank you. Thank you. You don't know what this means to me… and my mum.'

Outside, in the holding area, we were given forms to fill in with our details, including date of birth. I suddenly remembered that we were supposed to be over 16 to be in the competition, so Rachel and I adjusted our birth dates by three years. So far, no one had even hinted that we looked too young.

When we handed in the forms, we asked what would happen next.

'Well, the local auditions are still being held all over the country,' we were told. 'The next round will be held in November at a London hotel. But you'll get a letter explaining all about it.'

I wondered how I was going to break the news to my parents. How would they react? Would they actually let me go on to the next round? It would be typical of Mum to tell me I couldn't.

As we got ready to leave, Lauren said to Rachel, 'I'm really sorry to hear about your mum.' She was startled when Rachel and I both burst out laughing.

'There's nothing wrong with my mum,' said Rachel. 'I just said it because I was desperate to make them hear us. And it worked, didn't it?'

'Careful,' I said, because there were still lots of people around.

Lauren looked anxious. 'If they find out you lied to them, they'll disqualify us.'

'I don't care if they do,' said Rachel, 'as long as we get on TV, and get noticed. There's no such thing as bad publicity – isn't that what people say?'

****

I thought I would be in trouble for being late home from school – it was almost seven o'clock when I got off the bus. But I soon saw that my parents had something else to think about. A group of neighbours were standing outside our front door, arguing with Dad. One or two of them carried large signs with slogans on them: *No to Homeless Centre!*

Not wanting to get involved, I slipped round the side of the house and went in by the back door. I was surprised to find Mum sitting alone in the kitchen. It was nearly dark by now, but she hadn't put the light on. She was just sitting there.

'Are you all right, Mum?'

She didn't really answer me. 'Oh dear,' she said, 'is that the time? I must get on.' Slowly she got up and put a saucepan on the stove. She didn't even ask me where I'd been all this time – which was weird.

It was also strange that she wasn't out there with Dad, backing him up like she always did. But Dad seemed to be managing all right on his own. When he came in, a few minutes later, he looked quite pleased with the way things had gone.

'I've arranged for a public meeting next week in the church hall,' he told us. 'It's a chance for everyone to put forward their point of view. I've promised that we won't go ahead without listening to what the neighbours have to say. I hope, in return, they'll listen to me. Maybe I can persuade them to be a little more open-minded.'

'Let's hope so,' said Mum, but she didn't sound very hopeful. The opposite, in fact. She sounded quite low.

What was the matter with her? Was she upset about the neighbours getting angry? Or had Dad done something to annoy her? I hoped not. I was secretly proud of the fact that my parents never argued – unlike other people's parents, who had flaming rows that ended up in the divorce court.

I wondered if Dad had noticed her mood. He vanished into his study and started phoning people. Mum went on stirring the soup, like some kind of housewife-robot.

This didn't seem the best time to tell her about *Starmakers*. I would wait until she was in a better mood – if she ever was.

I ought to be careful about what I told her. I needed to disguise the fact that I'd skipped school, and that I had met up with Rachel again. And also the fact that we were breaking the rules of the contest. Mum would hate all that, even more than she hated programmes like *Starmakers*.

This was starting to look quite awkward. Would I be able to get to the next round? By now, I really wanted to. I would have to make very careful plans.

12

Broad river

Of course, I told a few people – Charlie and Abena first of all, making them promise not to tell anyone else at church, in case Mum found out.

'But your mum will have to know,' said Charlie. 'Otherwise, how are you going to get to London for the next round?'

'I'm going to tell her, of course,' I said. 'I just want to pick the right moment.'

'What will you do if she says you can't go?' asked Abena.

'She won't say that,' said Charlie. 'She couldn't. Could she?'

'I'm not sure,' I said. 'She won't like Rachel being involved, I do know that.'

Abena gave me a look that meant she might agree with Mum on this. But she was eager to know all the details of the audition. So were the girls in my class, when I told them. A few of them didn't believe me, until I showed them the official *Starmakers* number that had been pinned on my shirt.

'5,872. My lucky number,' I said.

'Sing us what you sang at the audition,' said Bindi.

'No. You'll have to wait until our single is released.'

I was joking, but Sophie obviously thought I was showing off. She said, 'But you can't even sing!'

'You're right. That's the crazy thing,' I said. 'We had one person who looked good but sounded awful, one who sounded great but didn't look it, and one who looked bad and sounded bad – which was me. It was a laugh, though… I enjoyed it.'

It's funny, but people are more impressed if you put yourself down than if you go around boasting. They like you better, too.

Miss Merton, the French teacher, had come in. She was trying, without much success, to make people sit down so that the lesson could start. We ignored her and went on talking.

'Can we come along and support you?' asked Sophie.

'Yeah, sure, if you can get to London. I'll let you know when the next round starts.'

Bindi said, 'Maybe you could get us tickets to be in the audience.'

'I don't think there is an audience for the next round,' I said. 'It's in a hotel, not a studio. But I'll find out.'

'Girls!' the teacher shouted. 'Will you please sit down!'

'Can't you see we're talking?' said Sophie cheekily.

'I don't want to have to tell you again!' She was getting cross now. Her cheeks were bright red.

'Oh… temper, temper,' I said, and everyone laughed.

We sat down when we were ready. I thought how nice it was to be admired by girls like Sophie and

Bindi – the liveliest, most popular girls in the class. I was in with the in-crowd now, all right.

At The Garret on Sunday, I wished I could tell everyone about *Starmakers*. But they would know soon enough when they saw me on TV. It would be quite a shock to most of them, especially the ones who only knew me as Eunice.

Awaking from my daydreams, I realised that Mark was talking about rules again. He said that the Ten Commandments could be summed up in just two:

Love God with all your heart and mind and strength.

Love your neighbour as much as you love yourself.

I could guess what the rest of his talk would be about, because I'd heard it all before. Who is your neighbour? Well, it's everyone actually, everyone in the entire world, even your enemies (like in the Good Samaritan story – another one that I've heard about a million times since I was a kid).

I decided to stir things up a bit.

'When it says *Love God with all your heart...*' I said, 'how do we know which god? I mean, there are lots of gods in the world – Allah and Krishna and so on – as well as the Christian God. How are we supposed to decide which one to follow?'

Mark looked surprised. (So did a few other people. After all, Eunice, the vicar's daughter, wasn't supposed to come out with questions like that.) At first he seemed lost for an answer. This wasn't part of his pre-planned talk.

Mary, the other youth leader, tried to help him out. She said, 'That's an interesting question. There is one important difference between Christianity and other faiths. Anyone know what it is?'

No one could tell her. She said, 'Most of the world's religions tell people about ways to please their gods – by keeping rules, or giving offerings, or meditating, or whatever. But Christians believe that's impossible. No one can keep God's laws perfectly. God is too high above us – we can never reach up to him.

'But he reached down to us. He sent Jesus into the world – his only son. Jesus said, *I am the way. Nobody can come to the Father, except through me.*'

It was strange. I had pretty well stopped believing in God, but when I heard the name of Jesus, I felt a kind of longing deep inside me... Perhaps it was just the memory of my childhood, when Dad or Mum would read me bedtime stories from the Bible. In those days, of course, I believed everything I was told.

Mark said, 'So, what did Jesus mean when he said we can come to the Father through him?'

'Jesus died to save us,' said Abena.

'That's right. He was perfect – he always followed God's laws. But when he died, he took on himself the punishment for all our law-breaking. If we trust in him, it's like all the wrong we've ever done is just wiped away and forgotten. That's how we can come to know God as our Father.'

Mary said, 'A father isn't someone high up and far away. He's close to us. He loves us...'

At this point I stopped listening. It was like a CD that I'd heard too many times. But that same night, I had a dream.

I was standing on the bank of an enormous, dirty brown river, so wide that the opposite shore was hidden in mist. There were lots of other people on the bank, some of them arguing about the best way to cross the river, others saying that there was no point even trying. 'It's not a river, it's the sea,' some of them said. 'There is no opposite bank. There aren't even any islands out there – it's empty.'

While they argued, I went to look at the river. The brown water was filthy. It stank of chemicals and sewage.

'Where has all this pollution come from?' I asked an old man.

'From us. From everyone.'

The water level seemed to be slowly rising. It rippled closer to my feet. Then, looking out through the yellow mist that lay on the surface, I thought I saw a movement.

'What's that? It looks like a boat coming in,' I said.

'It is a boat. It sails across to the other side, every day,' the old man said.

'Then why doesn't everyone get on it? Is it expensive?'

'No, it's free, they say. But when you get on board, the captain's in charge. You have to do what the captain says. And some people don't like that.'

'This captain,' I said, 'what's his name?'

But then I woke up to the sound of my alarm going off.

Weird dream, I thought. I remembered every detail, which I don't normally do. Feeling sluggish and slow, as if the brown river had invaded my mind, I got ready to face another Monday.

13

Not worth the risk

'We have to make plans,' said Rachel. 'Decide what we're going to wear, and all that. It's so exciting!' And she hugged herself tightly, as if the excitement was about to make her explode into a thousand pieces.

The letter had come through, giving us the dates for the next round – 20 and 21 November, at the Palmerston Hotel, West Kensington. It was still weeks away, but the three of us had got together to talk about it. We were at Rachel's house after school, on Lauren's day off. This was fine with Greta, the housekeeper. She was eager to help Rachel get on *Starmakers*.

'Have you told your parents?' I asked Rachel.

'Yes, and they weren't too thrilled. It's so unfair! If I'd managed to get onto *University Challenge*, they'd be boasting about it to everyone they know.'

'What about school? Can you get the time off?' asked Lauren. (The next stage was on a Tuesday and Wednesday.)

Rachel said, 'The school isn't too keen either. *Starmakers* is such a Highfield type of programme... not. But as long as my parents give permission, they can't stop me.'

I said, 'Didn't you get into trouble for skipping school on the audition day?'

'Oh, Greta sorted all that out. She wrote me a note. But what about your mum – have you told her yet?'

'No,' I admitted. 'I just haven't found the right moment. She's in a funny sort of mood these days.'

'What kind of mood?' asked Lauren.

'Depressed. No energy. I even thought she might be ill. But if I ask her, she always says there's nothing wrong.'

'So why don't you tell her about *Starmakers*?' asked Lauren. 'It might cheer her up.'

Rachel and I both laughed. 'You don't know my mum,' I said.

Maybe I should tell Dad, and get him to break the news to Mum. But Dad and Mum still weren't getting on too well. When Dad tried to talk to Mum, she gave him short, sharp answers. It was almost as if they'd had an argument – and because they never argued, they didn't know how to handle it.

Neither did I. The only thing I could do was to try and pretend that everything was normal. And from the outside, we probably did look normal… the vicar, his wife and daughter; a nice, cosy little family. Like a house on the edge of an earthquake zone, with the cracks only visible on the inside.

Lauren said, 'We really need to practise our singing.'

'How?' asked Rachel. 'We don't know what they're going to ask us to sing in the next round.'

'That doesn't matter. We can still practise. I mean we really weren't that great at the audition, were we?'

'We only got through because of me,' said Rachel, looking pleased with herself.

'Right,' Lauren said. 'But you won't be able to do that every time. So we'd better practise.'

It was lucky Rachel's room was at the top of the house, because the noises we made... well, let's just say, if you wanted soothing background music, you wouldn't pick a Last Minute CD.

'Rachel,' said Lauren, 'do try and listen to what other people are singing, and keep in tune with them. And Emma, you could sing out more. I can hardly hear you.'

'It's not my fault if I'm not musical,' Rachel complained.

After a while she got bored, and went back to discussing what we should wear. We needed clothes that would look sexy, suit all of us, make Lauren look younger and Rachel and me look older... not easy.

We decided to go shopping on Lauren's next day off. Fortunately, it was a busy weekend for babysitters – we'd had several replies to our ad at the shop – so I should have some money to spend.

***

My Friday sit had been booked by a man. This was quite unusual – it was mostly mums who called us. He explained that he was a single parent with a son aged 5.

He didn't ask me any of the questions that mothers usually asked, or even enquire how much I charged. He just gave me a time and an address. He lived in quite a posh part of Birton; Mum looked impressed as she dropped me off at the house.

But the man who let me in was not impressive. He was small and balding and looked about 60, quite old to have a 5-year-old son. That was the first thing that struck me as strange.

The second was that he didn't do the usual guided tour, showing me the child's bedroom and so on. And also, he didn't seem in any hurry to go out.

'Sit down, my dear,' he said. 'Let me get you a drink. What will you have?'

I asked for a Coke. When he brought it, he sat down on the sofa, rather closer than I liked. He asked me my name, and what I was doing at school. By now I was starting to think he was a bit creepy.

'Where's your little boy?' I asked him.

'Oh, he's asleep upstairs. He's very good, normally. He won't disturb us.' And he shifted himself a little closer, so that his leg was touching mine. 'How old did you say you were, Emma?'

'Nearly 14. Er… I'd really like to see your little boy, and make sure he's all right.' I said this because I was starting to suspect that the child didn't actually exist.

'No, no, he's fine. We don't want to wake him,' the man said. 'Would you like another drink?'

'Yes please.' Anything to give me a bit of time to think. What should I do? Make a run for it? But perhaps I'd got it all wrong – I'd look a total idiot.

He brought another glass of Coke. At least it looked like Coke. What if he had spiked my drink?

Now that I thought about it, the last drink had tasted slightly odd...

I went into total panic mode. Jumping up off the sofa, I gabbled, 'Really sorry – got to go – I just remembered I've got another booking somewhere else. Bye!' And I made for the door.

Once I was out in the street, I started feeling a bit of a fool. Probably I'd made a big mistake. The man was just being friendly... a bit too friendly, perhaps, but harmless...

Oh well, better safe than sorry, as Mum often said. It was a long way to walk home, and getting dark, so I rang her.

Mum took the whole thing seriously. 'You did the right thing,' she said as I got into the car. 'I wonder if we should tell the police about this. How did that man get your number? He's not a church member, is he?'

I explained about the ad in the shop window. Fortunately she didn't get too mad at me.

'Oh, Eunice, I did *tell* you. Didn't I? Only sit for people we know?'

'Yes,' I muttered.

'It's just not worth the risk. Maybe you can see that now.' She put her arm around me. 'Anyway, you're all right – that's the main thing.'

I leaned against her like I used to when I was little, remembering that safe, protected feeling... Mum's here, nothing can hurt me.

'I know you don't like it when we tell you what to do and what not to do,' she said. 'But there's always a reason for it. And the main reason is that we love you. We want to make sure you're all right.'

****

Mum and I felt closer than we had been for ages. I decided this was a good time to tell her about *Starmakers*.

She was quite surprised. For a moment she said nothing, and I could tell she was looking at the idea from all angles. *What would people think? The vicar's daughter appearing on a Saturday night TV show? Some people might be shocked, others impressed.*

'So you don't mind?' I said.

'Well, that depends. I don't particularly like the programme – it gives people silly ideas. Everyone seems to want to be famous these days, but we can't all be stars of stage and screen, can we? Promise me you won't get carried away?'

'I won't. Actually, I don't think we're very good. We won't get beyond the next round.'

I felt relieved – she seemed to have taken it all right. But that was because I'd been careful. I hadn't mentioned Rachel's name, or the school hours I'd missed and would need to miss for the next round.

It was good that I'd managed to tell her, because in a couple of weeks, the new *Starmakers* series would begin. Of course, they couldn't televise all the auditions – they would select a few of the best and worst to feature on the programme. Rachel and Lauren were hoping we would be included; I was hoping the opposite. But if we did appear, it wouldn't come as a total shock to my parents.

Let me rephrase that. It might be a total shock, but at least it wouldn't be a surprise.

14

Bunking off

The next time I bunked off school to meet up with Rachel, I nearly got into trouble. My form teacher, who had ticked off my name at registration, was asked to cover for the French teacher later that morning. (Miss Merton had 'gone off sick', or more likely bunked off, too.) He noticed that I wasn't there, and asked about it the next day.

'I had a dentist's appointment,' I told him.

'Have you got a note? If you leave during school hours, you're supposed to bring a note signed by your parent or guardian.'

'Oh, sorry. I didn't know.'

So I wrote my own note, printed it off on the computer during ICT, and forged Mum's signature. The forgery wasn't brilliant, but then how was Mr Gerard to know that? He seemed quite happy with the letter when I gave it to him the following day.

By now, at school, lots of people had heard about my *Starmakers* audition. They all had questions to ask. What was it like behind the scenes? Was Tony Stewart as sexy/as mean as he looked on TV? When would the audition be televised?

I enjoyed the attention. I knew it might not last too long – not if people actually saw our performance.

Abena said, 'You know Yao, my brother's friend? He asked me for your phone number. Want me to give it to him?'

'If you like,' I said, trying to sound casual. After the party I'd thought Yao might try to get in touch, but I wasn't too surprised when nothing happened – he did have a girlfriend already.

But that had been weeks ago. Why was he asking for my number now?

'Wait a minute. Did you tell him about *Starmakers*?' I asked.

'Kwami told him. I know you said not to tell anyone, but…'

'Oh, that doesn't matter now. You can tell anyone you like – Mum knows all about it. But listen – don't give Yao my number.'

'Why not? I thought you liked him.'

'He's not really interested in me. If he only wants to know me because I might be on TV, he can forget it.'

When I told Rachel about this, she thought I was crazy. 'But that's the whole point of being famous. Having everyone wanting to meet you, and every boy in the entire country dying to ask you out. You should make the most of it.'

She was in a fever of excitement about the next round of the contest. She kept changing her mind about clothes and hairstyles – every time she called me, she had a different idea. And she spent ages watching the video of the last *Starmakers* series, trying to work out why some people got chosen and others rejected. What were the judges really looking for?

I said, 'The people who get shown on TV are the really brilliant ones or the absolutely awful ones. I don't think we're ever going to be brilliant. So maybe we should concentrate on being terrible.'

'You're not taking this seriously,' Rachel complained. 'Listen, are you absolutely sure you're going to be allowed to come to the next round? Your mum won't kick up a fuss and say you can't go?'

'She seems okay with it at the moment.' Actually, we hadn't talked about it much. This was unusual – Mum would normally have wanted to know all the details of what I was planning to do. But she was still feeling low. All her energy seemed to have leaked away somehow, like air from a wrinkled balloon left outside after a party.

'Lauren thinks we ought to have a reserve ready in case one of us can't make it,' said Rachel. 'She's got a friend who's a really good singer, she says.'

'That's not a bad idea. Any of us could get ill,' I said.

So the next time we got together to practise, Lauren brought along her friend Keeley. It was true she was a good singer – much better than me – but she was also badly overweight. I saw Rachel looking at the two of us, and I could guess what was going through her mind. Plump Keeley, with the voice of a nightingale, or slim Emma, with the voice of a sparrow? If she decided Keeley would have a better chance with the judges, Rachel wouldn't think twice about ditching me. She was quite ruthless when it came to getting what she wanted.

****

Charlie and Abena dragged me along to the public meeting about the homeless project. Dad had asked for everyone who supported the idea to come along, so that he wouldn't be meeting the NIMBY neighbours all on his own.

I was amazed at how many church members turned up. Dad had persuaded a lot of people that his plan was a good one. The Parish Church Council had approved it. But would he be able to convince the neighbours?

First of all, he gave everyone a chance to speak out. Different people took turns to say what they thought – for or against. Even Charlie got up to speak.

'Why are you so scared of homeless people?' she asked. 'They're not all criminals or drunks. They're people. People who have got off the right track somehow. Maybe it's not their fault. But how are they ever going to get back to living a normal life, unless they get some help?'

I knew she was thinking about her brother when she said it. She sounded so emotional that everyone listened, and some people applauded.

Dad said, 'Charlie is absolutely right. Homeless people are often caught in a trap. No one will give them a job because they don't have a fixed address. But they can't rent a room because they're not earning a living. And they start to feel that no one cares about them. We've all turned our backs on them; we all ignore them. Society has given up on them and hardly even sees them as human.

'I'm not saying that we can solve their problems, just by providing a day centre. And some do have serious problems, I realise that. But at least we can show that not everyone hates them just because they are homeless. And perhaps we can try to show them that there is a way out of the homelessness trap. If people want to get out of it, we can help them.'

'That's all well and good,' said an elderly lady, 'but I still say you shouldn't be starting a scheme like that here. You are lowering the tone of the area.'

'I'm trying to sell my house at the moment,' a man said. 'What are potential buyers going to think? I could lose a lot of money.'

The discussion went on for ages. At last Dad said, 'What I would like to suggest is a trial scheme. The centre would be open for just one or two days a week. After a month or so, we would review it, and see if it was causing serious problems to residents. If it was, we would close it down. On that basis, how many people would feel able to support our project?'

A lot of people put their hands up – including most of the residents. A few still looked hostile.

'Go ahead, then,' said the leader of the residents' group. 'But if there are problems – and there will be, believe me – you haven't heard the last of us.'

So that was how it ended. The scheme would go ahead, for a trial period at least.

As people left the hall, I helped Dad to put the chairs away. 'I still can't believe you managed to persuade those people,' I said to him. 'How did you do it?'

'With a lot of prayer beforehand,' he said. 'And by remembering that NIMBYs are people, too. It's not only homeless people who go off the right track.'

'What do you mean?'

'Well, I'd say there are some people in this street who are very unhappy. They don't believe in God, so they have other priorities like money, or the right public image, or whatever. But that kind of thing can never satisfy people for long.'

Did he mean this for me? I wasn't sure, so I said nothing.

'I'd like to show them that there is a way back,' he said. 'Whoever we are, whatever we've done, there's always a way back to God, and he's ready to meet us. Ready to welcome us home.'

He put the lights out and locked the doors of the hall. 'Come on then, let's get back and see how your mother is.'

Mum hadn't attended the meeting – she had a headache, she said. Bunking off, more likely, I thought. By the time we got home, she had gone to bed, and the house was in darkness.

15

They can't stop me

When we lived in the village, I used to work quite hard at school, always getting homework in on time and all that stuff. I used to read a lot, too, and spend hours practising my cello; in Nembury there wasn't much else to do. Most of the time, teachers liked me and thought of me as one of the clever ones. But I hardly had any friends.

So, when we moved, I told myself it wasn't smart to be too clever. I would rather be noticed for my looks and personality. Most of the time, I did just enough work to get by, without getting into trouble.

Mum sometimes looked at my homework and told me off for being slapdash and lazy. 'You were doing better work than this in Year 7,' she said.

'Yes, well, in those days I was a bit of a boff.'

'A what?'

'A swot,' I translated for her into the language of her childhood. 'And I'm not any more. I have friends now.'

She looked worried. She had obviously liked it better in the days when I was getting top marks for schoolwork and zero for social skills. (Was that what she had been like at my age?)

After half-term there was a parents' evening at school – a chance for our parents to meet the teachers and find out how we were getting on in Year 9. I never used to mind this kind of thing at my old

school, because I always got good reports.
Intelligent... hard-working... rather quiet, but very
well-behaved...

This time I had the feeling things weren't going to
be so good. And I was right.

The first shock for Mum and Dad was finding out
that I had changed my name. When the Science
teacher started talking about me as Emma, I could see
that they thought he'd made a mistake. Especially
when he said I was lazy and didn't concentrate in
lessons.

'Er... excuse me, but this is Eunice, not Emma,' said
Mum. 'Eunice Todd.'

The teacher looked equally surprised. I quickly
explained that my first name was Eunice, but
everyone at school called me Emma.

'Well, as I was saying, your daughter needs to pull
her socks up. She's clearly intelligent, but she has
wasted a lot of time this term. She has only completed
about half her assignments, and if she carries on like
this, her grades are going to be very disappointing.'

It was the same in almost every subject. Then we
came to Mr Gerard, my form teacher.

'I'm afraid I've heard reports from Emma's French
teacher that she is part of a group of girls being
disruptive in class. I'm also a bit concerned that
Emma has been absent several times, once for an
entire day, without a covering letter,' he said. (Now it
was my turn to be shocked. I didn't think anyone had
noticed until the last time I tried it.) 'And when I

asked for a letter, she gave me this. Did you write it, Mrs Todd?'

Mum looked hard at my absence letter, and the forged signature. 'I most certainly didn't,' she said. 'I can't even use a computer. Eunice, did you make this up?'

There was no point trying to deny it. I got a severe telling-off from Mr Gerard, and a worse one from Mum when we got home. She was absolutely furious. Dad didn't say much, but I knew he was hurt and disappointed. I had let him down... let both of them down.

'You're grounded for a week,' Mum told me.

I tried not to look relieved. A week didn't matter – the next round of *Starmakers* was still two weeks off.

Dad said, 'What happened, Eunice? It seems you've changed in the last six months. You always used to get such good reports, but now...'

'It was the move that did it,' Mum said to Dad. Her voice was angry and bitter. 'The new school. Bad influences. I wish we'd stayed in Nembury! We should never have come here!'

There – she had finally come out and said it.

I don't know what Dad would have said, because she didn't wait for him to reply. She stormed out of the room.

****

Two days later, Mum still hadn't got over her disappointment in me. I saw her looking at me now and then, as if I'd suddenly turned into a complete stranger. Who was this Emma person? What had happened to Eunice, the daughter she knew and loved?

It was Saturday night. I was keen to see *Starmakers* in case they showed our audition, but that meant Mum would be watching it too. Not for the first time, I wished I had my own TV in my bedroom.

Mum was busy with her sewing, hardly noticing what was on TV. But she looked up when she heard my gasp of excitement.

'It's us! We're on TV!'

To my surprise, Mum jumped up and went to tell Dad. (Normally, she never disturbed him when he was preparing his Sunday sermons.) He came hurrying out of his study. So they both saw a bit of our disastrous first appearance.

I had managed to make myself forget just how awful we had been. It was embarrassing to be reminded. I wanted to cover my ears and hide under the sofa. Mum and Dad watched in horrified fascination.

'Don't say it,' I begged them. 'We were terrible, I know. But it did get better…'

The judges gave their verdict, and then Rachel made her desperate plea. The camera zoomed in on her anguished face. 'It's for my mum… she's got cancer… they say she won't live until Christmas…'

'Isn't that Rachel Collins?' Dad said suddenly.

I had hoped he wouldn't realise it was her with her hair so short. Maybe it was her voice that he recognised, or her huge eyes, brimming with fake tears.

'Rachel? You've got together with Rachel again?' Mum was furious. 'We told you to stay away from her! If I'd known she was involved in this—'

'What was that she said about her mother having cancer?' asked Dad.

'Oh, it's not true,' I said. 'Rachel wanted the judges to give us another chance, and they did – look.'

On screen, we were singing again and sounding better. But Mum snatched up the remote and switched us off in mid-verse. She was extremely angry.

'There. What did I tell you about bad influences? That Rachel girl would do anything, absolutely anything, to get attention. I won't have you associating with her, Eunice. You are not to take any further part in that programme.'

****

'And she really means it?' asked Sophie, at school. 'But that's so unfair!'

'Haven't you tried to argue with her?' said Bindi.

'Of course I've tried. I thought Dad might be on my side, but he agreed with Mum. And when she says "No means no!" there's no point arguing any more. You might as well argue with a stone wall.'

'Well, if it was me,' said Lucy, 'nothing would stop me getting on *Starmakers*. I mean, it's a once-in-a-lifetime chance. Never mind what they say – you should still go.'

Sophie said, 'Yeah. Get up early, slip out before they're awake, and get on that London train. By the time they find out, it will be too late.'

I was coming around to that idea myself. Why did Mum always have to spoil everything, with her stupid rules and impossibly high standards? She would ruin my life if I let her. She would make me old before my time, like she was.

Mum had forbidden me to contact Rachel again, except for one phone call to tell her that I wouldn't be going to London. But of course I did ring her when Mum wasn't around.

Rachel said, 'I think your mum's being totally stupid. Why is she so mad at you? If anyone should get mad, it should be my mum, not yours.'

'Oh, yes... what did she say when she found out?'

'She wasn't exactly pleased. People have been ringing her up, full of sympathy. How terrible... we didn't know you were ill... is there anything we can do?' She giggled. 'Mum thinks if the TV people find out what I did, we'll get disqualified. But she's not going to stop me competing. She knows how much it means to me.'

'Yeah, well my mum's not going to stop me competing, either. I don't care what she says – I am going to London. I don't want to let you and Lauren down.'

So we started making plans.

'We have to be at the London hotel for eleven o'clock,' said Rachel. 'And if we're late, the letter says, we won't be allowed in. Lauren's been looking up train times. She says there's a train that leaves Birton at 8.15.'

The main line station was a half-hour bus ride away from my house. I'd better check the bus timetable. I would have to be up pretty early, to get out of the house before my parents woke at 7.

'I hope you can make it,' said Rachel. 'Just in case, Keeley's going to come along too. I mean, obviously, if you can get there, we'd rather have you. But in case your mum finds out and stops you…'

'She won't,' I said. 'Nothing's going to stop me – I promise.'

16
Too late

Rachel gave me some good advice. 'Don't tell anyone what you're planning to do. And act like you're really upset with your parents – you know, give them the silent treatment, or moan at them every now and then. If you seem too happy, your mum's going to get suspicious.'

So I didn't even tell Abena and Charlie. They tried to cheer me up by telling me that Last Minute wouldn't get any further than the next round, in any case. (Most people who had seen us on TV would probably agree.)

'Anyway, I don't see what's so great about being famous,' said Abena. 'It doesn't make people happy, that's obvious.'

She flicked through one of Charlie's mum's magazines, pointing out all the celebrities with problems. The rock star going through a bitter divorce... the drug-addict actress... the England footballer exposed for taking bribes... the alcoholic MP...

Charlie said, 'The newspapers love that kind of thing. Whenever a celebrity does something wrong, even just driving too fast, it's in all the papers.'

'Yeah, it's like they build people up and then, when they're famous, knock them down again.'

'It's Rachel who needs to hear this, not me,' I said.

****

On Friday, Rachel rang me to arrange an extra practice session.

'Tomorrow night?' I was taken aback. 'I can't. I'm supposed to be babysitting.'

I expected her to be mad at me. She never liked it if people didn't fit in with her plans. But she took the news quite calmly.

'If you can't make it, don't worry. Keeley can stand in for you.'

'No – wait a minute. I'll see if I can do a swap.'

Abena already had a booking for Saturday, so I rang Charlie. She didn't particularly want to swap with me, but after a bit of persuasion, she agreed.

'Why do you need a swap, anyway?' she asked.

'Something's come up,' I said evasively.

'Have you got a date? Let me guess – Yao asked you out.'

I didn't answer.

'Okay, don't tell me then. But you owe me one for this.' She sounded cross, but I didn't care.

The practice went well. We sorted out the final details. Now we wouldn't have to meet again until Tuesday morning, at Birton station.

On Monday night, I put all my things in a backpack. Then I set my alarm clock and put it under my pillow so that it wouldn't wake my parents. Actually I didn't need the alarm – I was too wired with excitement to sleep much. By 6am I was up and dressed, ready to go.

Should I leave a message for my parents? I couldn't decide. In the end I scribbled a note and left it on my pillow. *Gone to London, back tomorrow night.* They would know why I'd gone, but not exactly where. Once I was on my way, they wouldn't be able to catch me.

The tricky bit was getting out of the house, and I held my breath as I crept downstairs. But there wasn't a sound except for the ticking of the clock in the hall. I quietly unlocked the door and slipped out.

It was still dark outside, and very cold. There was plenty of time, so instead of waiting at the bus stop nearest to home, I started walking. The first bus of the day swept past me between stops, brightly lit and quite empty. It didn't matter. I wasn't due to meet my friends until eight o'clock on Platform 4.

By 7, when Mum would be getting up and finding my bed empty, I was safely on a bus. My phone rang at exactly 7.02 – I didn't answer it because I could see who was calling. Mum left an angry message on my voicemail. Then she rang again, twice, without leaving a message, and after that she gave up.

I reached the station in good time and queued for my ticket, which was horrendously expensive. (We would be claiming the money back from the TV company, so I couldn't buy a child's ticket.)

I was on the platform ten minutes early. No sign of the others. There should be four of them – Rachel, Lauren, Keeley and Greta, the housekeeper. Rachel's parents had told her she could only go to London if an adult went too. (They didn't seem to count Lauren, aged 25, as an adult.) And Greta had volunteered at once.

I walked restlessly up and down. By 8.05 the others still hadn't appeared, and the 8.15 London train had come up on the screen as the next to arrive at Platform 4. Feeling anxious, I texted Rachel. *Where R U?*

She rang me back at once. 'We're on the train. What happened? Did your mum find out?'

'What do you mean you're on the train?' I said, bewildered. 'It hasn't come in yet. I'm waiting on the platform, like you said.'

'Oh… didn't you get my message? We decided to get an earlier train in case there were any hold-ups. I left a message on your mobile last night to be there at 7.'

'But I checked for messages before I went to bed. I'm sure I did, I always do. Why didn't you ring me this morning when you saw I wasn't there?'

Rachel said, 'I thought your mum must have stopped you from coming. Or else you'd decided not to risk it. Look, I'm really sorry…'

The London train was pulling into the station with a hiss of brakes. People moved towards the platform edge.

'What am I supposed to do, then?' I said frantically. 'Should I get on the next train?'

'That's up to you. If you do, we'll wait for you at King's Cross – where's a good place to wait, Greta? – outside WHSmith at King's Cross. OK?'

'OK.'

Lauren's voice came on the phone. 'We'll wait as long as we can, Emma, but if your train gets held up, we'll have to go. You know what they said in the letter – be at the hotel by 11 or they won't let you in. We just can't risk that happening.'

Rachel said, 'So if we're not there, follow us to the hotel.'

'I can't!' I said, panicking now. 'I don't know how to get there! You've got the letter with the address.'

'It's the Palmerston Hotel, remember? Two minutes from West Kensington tube station.'

People were coming off the train and others were starting to get on. What should I do? Go or stay? Even if I went straight home, I would still be in trouble, and all for nothing…

The doors began to slam, like a slow handclap. I got onto the train and found a seat. I was feeling terrified – I'd never been on a journey like this on my own.

The worst thing was, I didn't know what to believe. Had Rachel really left me a message last night? I was 99 per cent certain she hadn't. Perhaps she'd called the wrong number and left a message for completely the wrong person.

Or perhaps she was lying. She had decided Keeley would be better than me, so she'd arranged for me to get the wrong train. They would all go off to the hotel, leaving me in London, lost and alone…

I texted Rachel. *Am on train. CU Kings X.* Then all I could do was sit there, willing the train to go faster. I had an ache in my stomach, partly from anxiety, partly because there hadn't been time for breakfast. I bought a sandwich from the buffet, but couldn't eat it.

The journey seemed to take years. Stop, start… stop, start… workmen on the line… wait in a station for ages… start again, stop again… At last there was an announcement. 'This train will be 40 minutes late arriving at London King's Cross due to work on the line. We apologise for the delay.'

I rang Rachel to tell her, but I couldn't get through. They might already be on the underground. Perhaps they hadn't even bothered to wait, but had gone straight to the hotel. How was I supposed to get there all on my own?

It was 10.30 when my train finally arrived. As I expected, there was no one waiting outside WHSmith. They might at least have left Greta there to make sure I was all right. They didn't care at all! They probably wanted me to give up and get the next train home!

I hurried towards the information centre, queued up impatiently, and asked how to get to West Kensington tube station. I was given a map and some directions. It wasn't my first visit to London – but it was my first time on my own, and even with the map, I got very confused. Somehow I got onto the wrong branch of the District Line, ending up in Wimbledon. I had to change trains twice before I finally got there.

Even before I saw the hotel name, I knew I'd come to the right place. There were two huge trucks parked outside, labelled with the name of the TV company, and a crowd of onlookers waiting to catch a glimpse of someone famous.

I pushed my way through the crowd. The hotel entrance was guarded by half a dozen security men. It looked as if *Starmakers* had taken over the entire hotel. Ordinary members of the public weren't being allowed in – but then I wasn't an ordinary person.

'I'm one of the contestants,' I told the guards.

'Sorry,' he said. 'You should have been here before 11, so we can't let you in. Those are the rules.'

'But it's not my fault! My train was delayed! Please let me in. I'm part of a group, and the others are already here.'

The man looked doubtful. 'Let me see your official letter.'

'My friends have got it. We're in a band called Last Minute. Ask someone, if you don't believe me.'

'Wait there.' He went into the hotel foyer and talked to a woman with a clipboard. A minute later he was back.

'Last Minute are already signed in, three of them, plus their voice coach. All present and correct. Nice try, girl – but you can't come in.'

I attempted Rachel's trick of looking beautiful and desperate. 'Oh, please…' But I wasn't Rachel. I wasn't beautiful or desperate enough.

The guard said, 'Sorry, love. I've got a daughter about your age, and she's just the same – dying to get in here and meet someone famous.'

'Why don't you wait outside?' another man said. 'You might see the judges arriving soon. But we can't let you in. That's the rules.'

17

Let me in

Steaming with fury, I rang Rachel. Surprise, surprise – I couldn't get through.

'Rachel! I'm outside and they won't let me in. Do something!' I told her voicemail. Then I texted Lauren, and I would have called Keeley and 'voice coach' Greta, if only I had their numbers.

'They might have been told to switch their phones off, love,' said a woman standing nearby. I looked round, and realised that the whole crowd had been watching my little drama. Some of them were grinning broadly.

This shouldn't be happening! I ought to be inside the hotel with the others, practising, preparing to meet the judges. Instead, fat Keeley had taken my place – was she actually pretending to be 16-year-old Emma? Did she think anyone would believe her?

And I was stuck outside. Out in the cold, with all the no-hopers and celebrity watchers, who should have been nudging each other and saying, 'I've seen her on TV.'

There was nothing I could do except stand and wait. After a while, the security men made me move off the steps and join the crowd. A celebrity must be about to arrive.

It was Tony Stewart in a red Ferrari. The crowd, mostly made up of women, went crazy, pushing closer and shouting his name. But the security guards kept them out of Tony's way as he strolled into the hotel, smiling to himself. Then Kate arrived in a taxi. Soon after, Paul and Nicci, the bubbly blonde presenter, got out of a limo together.

'Oh yes, they're an item,' I heard someone say. 'Don't you ever read *Hello*?'

'But he must be three times her age! What on earth does she see in him?'

'Money, I suppose. A career. She would never have got the presenter's job if it wasn't for him.'

When they had gone in, the excitement died. A sort of sigh went through the crowd. There wouldn't be anyone to stare at now, not until the contestants started getting rejected by the judges. Some of the onlookers went away, but many of them stayed. *Get a life*, I wanted to tell them.

My phone rang. I was so sure it would be Rachel, I answered it without checking to see who was calling.

'It's only me,' said Dad. 'Did you get there safely? Are you all right?'

'Of course I'm all right,' I said crossly.

'Where are you?'

'The Palmerston Hotel in West Kensington.' Outside it, to be precise. But I wasn't going to tell Dad that.

'We were worried about you. But your mum rang Rachel's mother, and she said their housekeeper had gone with you. A very sensible woman, she said.'

'Yes. Look, Dad, you needn't worry – I'm okay.'

Dad said, 'We can't help worrying. You're our daughter and we love you. But Eunice, I'm very disappointed that you—'

'I have to go, Dad, we're rehearsing. Bye!'

If only it was as easy to avoid a telling-off face to face as it was on the phone! There would be serious trouble when I got home. I had always known that, but I thought it would be worth it to be on *Starmakers*. How stupid to get into trouble, and probably be grounded for ever, just so that I could stand outside a hotel all day.

Suddenly I had a thought. There might be another entrance which wasn't so well-guarded – a kitchen door or a fire escape or something.

I slipped through the crowd and strolled along the front of the hotel. There was an alley at the side, leading to a scruffy yard full of dustbins. The hotel had looked quite posh from the front, but from the back it wasn't so appealing. There was a smell of burnt pizza and rotting fruit.

I had been right – there was a fire escape, and no one seemed to be guarding it. I climbed the first flight of metal steps, but then I had to stop. The stairway was blocked by a steel-barred gate with no handle on my side.

Beyond the gate was a small balcony and another flight of steps. And on the balcony was Nicci, the *Starmakers* presenter, who seemed to have nipped out for a smoke. She stared at me through the metal grille.

'The paparazzi are getting younger all the time,' she said.

'I'm not from the papers,' I said indignantly. 'I'm a contestant, but the security men won't let me in.'

'Oh? Why not?'

I found myself telling her all about it, because I was so furious, and she seemed friendly. The missed phone call… the late train… the dumb security men… 'Can't you tell them to let me in?' I asked. 'Or you could open this gate for me.'

'Yes, of course. But before that, maybe you can help me. This girl Rachel – she's the one whose mother's ill, right? Tell me a bit more. What sort of cancer has she got?'

Oh help. I couldn't remember what Rachel had said. If I told Nicci the wrong thing, it would look very suspicious.

'I have a feeling she said lung cancer,' Nicci said helpfully.

'Yes, that's right. Lung cancer.'

'And she's really quite ill? Do you think she'd be well enough to be in the studio audience, if Rachel gets through to the final 15?'

'I'm not sure,' I said. 'You'd better ask Rachel, not me.'

'I don't want to upset her. You know, Rachel's made quite an impact on the viewers. We got lots of emails and phone calls after her first appearance. If she's one of the final 15, she'll pull in thousands of votes. It's such a sad story, and Rachel's only… how old?'

'Thir—' I began to say, but stopped in time. 'Er… 16, same as me.'

Nicci smiled. 'Thanks. You've been a great help.'

With a swift movement, she stubbed out her half-smoked cigarette. Then she swung round and disappeared into the building, leaving me outside the gate.

'Don't forget to tell them to let me in!' I called through the bars. But I had no way of knowing if she'd heard me.

I waited for a while, but no one came. Then I went back to the main entrance and waited some more. Finally, I asked the security man if Nicci Malone had sent a message about me. He shook his head, grinning.

By now I'd begun to feel uneasy. Why had Nicci been asking those questions? And what if Rachel gave her different answers from mine? I ought to warn her...

Walking away from the entrance, I tried to call her, but once again I could only leave a message. 'If anyone asks, say your mum has lung cancer. And she's very ill – much too ill to be filmed.'

But my warning might be too late. Last Minute could be getting their marching orders right now. And when Rachel played back my message, she'd think I was the one to blame. She would hate me for the rest of her entire life.

Had she ever liked me in the first place? I wasn't at all sure. Rachel wasn't a real friend – not like Charlie or Abena. They would never have treated me like this.

A ripple of excitement stirred the crowd by the entrance. Someone was coming out! I squeezed through to the front row to see who it was.

To my relief, it was the World's Ugliest Boy Band. They must have been rejected by the judges, but they stood on the steps, waving and smiling as if they'd won. This was the finish of their bid for stardom. They were making the most of the last few seconds, before they rejoined the crowd of ordinary people.

If Last Minute were to be disqualified, I definitely did not want to be there when they came out. Even if they were successful, I would never be part of their success. The day had been a complete and utter waste of time.

Should I go home? I really didn't want to – not yet. That would mean admitting what a washout the whole trip had been, and Mum would say 'I told you so' over and over again. Far better to go back tomorrow, like I'd originally planned. Then I could pretend that I'd enjoyed myself and it had all been worth it.

I thought I had enough money to pay for a night in a cheap hotel. But meanwhile, I was starving. It was four o'clock and I'd hardly had a thing to eat all day. The smell of food drew me along the road and round the corner, where I found a couple of takeaways.

'Chicken burger and chips, please. And a Coke.'

I took off my backpack to get my wallet out. Strange – the side pocket had come open. I usually kept it zipped up.

The pocket was empty. My mobile should have been in there, but it wasn't. Likewise my wallet, along with all my money and my ticket home. And even my glasses in their designer case. Gone... all gone.

18

Go home

The man in the shop didn't believe my money had been stolen. He wouldn't give me anything – not even a few chips.

'Always people want something for nothing. Am I the Oxfam? No. Am I the Social Services? No. Now get lost.'

'But I'm absolutely starving. I haven't eaten all day.'

'Same with hundreds of people. I can't feed all, can I?'

'I'll send you the money when I get home – I promise.'

'Ha. That's a good story. You got no home and no money. Foolish girl! Why do you run away from home? Go to your family – they can feed you.'

He thought I was a homeless runaway. And when I saw myself in the wall mirror, I understood why. The backpack, the pale, hungry face and the look of desperation…

Well, if I looked like a beggar, why not become one? I was so hungry, I was ready to try anything.

I stood in the street with my hand held out. Most people walked round me as if I was a lamppost, ignoring me. A few looked me in the face, glanced away, and walked past. Just one or two of them stopped.

'Please, I've had my money stolen and I'm hungry... 20p, that's all I'm asking for...'

This was hard work. After half an hour, I was sick of it. I had been lectured by an old lady, leered at by several men and totally ignored by almost everyone. It was getting dark and I was freezing... but at last I had enough to buy some food.

Because I was so hungry, the greasy chips tasted wonderful. But now I was thirsty. I would have to start begging again if I was to buy a drink, and what about getting home? It would take ages to collect enough money for a rail ticket.

'Go to your family,' the chip-shop man had said. I knew I could ring them from a call box any time, day or night. But my pride held me back. I didn't want my parents to come and rescue me as if I was a helpless child. Mum would never let me hear the end of it.

I got up and started begging again. The road was getting busier now as people came home from work; under the streetlights their faces looked grey and tired. Once again, most of them ignored me.

Was this what it would feel like to be homeless and jobless? I felt non-human. I felt like a cardboard cut-out figure outside a shop, to be avoided, or sworn at if someone bumped into it. People didn't see me as a real person with feelings, hopes and fears. They just saw one more scrounging beggar, out to get their money and give nothing in return.

Suddenly I remembered the homeless stranger on our doorstep. Now, like him, I was on the outside, and the people on the inside didn't care – didn't even want to look at us. They wanted to shut us out of their lives and lock the door.

By 7.30 I had collected about £5 in change – nowhere near enough for a hotel room or a rail ticket. It was freezing cold. My hands and feet were so chilled, I could hardly feel them.

Where was I going to spend the night? It looked as if I had two choices. Either go back to the Palmerston Hotel and try yet again to get in, or sleep on the street.

My stomach was curling up into a tight ball when I noticed a middle-aged man hanging around nearby, staring at me. Suddenly he smiled, showing a horrible set of yellowed teeth.

I turned my back on him and began to walk away, but a quick glance over my shoulder told me he was following me. I was starting to feel rather sick – sick and scared.

'Is he bothering you, miss?' It was an old man at a newspaper stall who spoke to me. I nodded.

'Leave the girl alone,' the old man said loudly.

People turned to look, and the toothy man, embarrassed, hurried away.

'Thank you,' I said gratefully.

The old man said, 'Don't thank me. Get out while you still can. I seen enough young girls like you messing up their lives, and I want to say to them all, go home. Just go home.'

'Yes, but…'

'I don't know or care what you done. Your family will have you back, if you ask them. Am I right? Go home, girl.'

Home… suddenly it was the one place in the world where I longed to be.

'There's a call box right over there,' the old man said.

I hurried across the road. Should I ring the house phone, and risk having Mum shout at me? No, Dad's mobile would be better. I knew the number off by heart, from the dozens of times I'd had to tell it to people when he was out.

What should I say? Dad, I'm really sorry… I didn't mean to upset you… I want to come home, but I can't, I've got no money…

I fed in the coins and dialled the number. He picked up the phone instantly.

'Dad, it's me, I'm really sorry—'

'Are you all right?' he interrupted. 'Tell me where you are. I'll come and get you.'

A feeling of relief washed over me. I'd hoped he would say that, even though it would be a long drive. Birton was over 100 miles away.

I said, 'I'm in London – West Kensington.'

'Yes, so am I. I'm outside the hotel.'

'What?'

'Outside the Palmerston Hotel. Where are you?'

'Just down the road and around the corner.' I couldn't quite believe he was so close. 'I'll be there in two minutes.'

I ran back towards the hotel. Our car was parked outside it, on a double yellow line. (Dad never parks on yellow lines.) As soon as he saw me, Dad got out and came hurrying to meet me. He gave me an enormous hug.

'Oh, Dad… oh, Dad… it's great to see you…'

'Good to see you, too,' said Dad. 'What on earth's been going on?'

'It's a long story… I'll tell you in the car.' I wanted to get away from the staring eyes of the crowd still gathered outside the hotel.

As we returned to the car, I asked Dad how he came to be in London.

'Well, I tried to ring you at about five o'clock, and a man's voice answered. When I asked to speak to you, he just laughed and rang off. That worried me. Your phone's been stolen, I take it?'

'Yes. Probably when I was standing in the crowd back there.' The thief could have unzipped my backpack, and I wouldn't have noticed a thing, surrounded by jostling people.

Dad said, 'So then I rang Rachel's parents and got a contact number for the housekeeper. But the woman said she hadn't actually seen you today because you'd missed the train. You had been outside the hotel earlier, she thought. You'd left a message for Rachel. But she had no idea where you were.

'By now, of course, we were anxious. I decided to drive down here to see if I could find out more. Your mother stayed at home, in case you rang there. I'd just got here when you called me.'

'Thanks, Dad. Thanks for coming all the way here.' I knew he hated motorway driving, especially in the dark. But for my sake, he hadn't thought twice about it.

'It was worth it to have you back, safe and sound.' He smiled at me. 'Come on – let's get you home.'

The car was lovely and warm inside. As we drove off, I looked back once, but no one was watching us. Nobody saw us go.

19

The homeward road

Dad handed me his mobile and told me to ring Mum, to let her know I was all right. As soon as she knew I was safe and well and on my way home, she started getting mad at me. I couldn't even say sorry – she wouldn't let me get a word in edgeways.

When she had put the phone down, Dad said, 'Remember, she's been anxious about you all day. So have I. What happened, exactly?'

I told him everything. It was easy to talk because he wasn't looking at me – he had to keep an eye on the traffic. But anyway, I knew he wouldn't yell at me, because Dad isn't like that.

'I'm sorry, Dad,' I said at the end. 'I didn't want to upset you. Or Mum.'

'So why did you disobey us?' he asked quietly.

'Because... I suppose because it meant a lot to me, being on *Starmakers*. Everyone at school was dead jealous. And they said how unfair it was, me not being allowed to go. But now I wish I hadn't gone. I've had a terrible day! I should have stayed at home!'

He said nothing, and I thought of the terrible day he must have had, worrying about me.

'I am sorry, Dad. I really mean that. I won't do it again.'

That made him smile. 'So you'll always do everything we ask you from now on? If so, you'll be a quite unusual teenager.'

'I will try, Dad. It's just that Mum... well, she's so strict about everything. You know – what I wear, what time I have to come home, and all that. It's like she wants me to be 100 per cent good and well behaved all the time. And I can't do it!'

'No,' he said thoughtfully. 'I don't think anyone could.'

'Well, can't you talk to her? Make her see that she doesn't have to be such a perfectionist all the time?'

'Yes, I'll try to have a word with her,' he said. He sounded discouraged, and I remembered that he and Mum weren't talking that much.

I was suddenly sick of the way we had all been acting – papering over the cracks, pretending things were fine at home when they weren't. I took a deep breath.

'Mum doesn't seem too happy at the moment,' I said.

He didn't answer. He was trying to get onto a busy roundabout, where a constant stream of headlights surged past, leaving no gaps. Was he going to try and ignore what I'd said?

I said, 'I don't think she's ever been happy since we moved. She liked it better in the country.'

Someone hooted behind us. Dad edged forwards slowly, and found a gap. Finally he spoke.

'I still think the move was the right thing to do. But I didn't realise it would mean such a drastic change for Marjorie. Maybe that was short-sighted of me. Leaving her friends behind, and all the things she used to do in the parish… She said the other day that she didn't feel needed at St Jude's.'

'Why not?'

'Well, the previous vicar was a woman. She didn't have a spouse who could organise the newsletter and the ladies' group and the flower rota and so on. So various people in the church took those jobs on, and they're still doing them. There's actually very little for Mum to do.'

I said, 'She always used to grumble about how much she had to do in Nembury. But she liked it really.'

'Yes, and it helped her to get to know people. I think she's feeling quite lonely in Birton.'

Perhaps Mum should get a job, I thought. But what job? She was 53 and had no experience of any kind of work, except being a vicar's wife. (In Nembury, she used to say that was a full-time job in itself, unfortunately with a salary of zero.)

That reminded me of something. Vicar's wife… marriage certificate…

'Dad,' I said, 'why didn't Mum want me to see your marriage certificate? I started looking at it a few weeks ago, but she snatched it away, and said it was none of my business. What was that all about?'

'I don't know,' said Dad, sounding puzzled. 'Oh! Yes. I do know, actually.' He stopped talking as another roundabout came up. I waited impatiently.

'Don't tell your mother we talked about this,' he said at last. 'She's very sensitive on the subject. But I'm going to tell you because really it's nothing you needn't know. And it may help you to understand her better.'

'I won't tell her,' I said.

'One of the things that's listed on a marriage certificate is the name of the bride's father. On ours, that space is blank, because Marjorie never knew who her father was. Her mother had an affair with a married man, and when Marjorie was born, her mother brought her up alone, as a single parent.'

'I don't understand. What's so terrible about that? Loads of people have single parents.'

'This was 50 years ago, remember. Things were different then. If your mother was unmarried, you were called 'illegitimate', and people looked down on you, as if it was your fault. All through your mum's childhood, she was conscious of being different. People disapproved of her. She was somehow not quite good enough.'

I said, 'So she's spent her whole life trying to get accepted. Trying to please people.'

'Yes, and in Nembury, most of the time, she succeeded. Everyone used to tell me how marvellous she was, and how lucky I was to have her. And they were right, of course,' he added as an afterthought.

'But now she feels no one needs her,' I said. 'The church doesn't, and I don't so much because I'm getting older. And you don't either, Dad. That's what she thinks.'

This idea startled Dad. He slowed down almost to a stop.

'Why do you say that?'

'You seem to be managing all right without her help. The new parish... the homeless project... Know what you ought to do, Dad? You ought to ask her if she'd help with the homeless centre.'

'She would never agree. She was against the idea right from the start,' he said.

'Yes, because she thought it would upset the neighbours. But you seem to have persuaded most of them. I bet you can persuade Mum, if you try. You ought to ask her, Dad.'

'Perhaps I ought,' he said doubtfully.

'What are you scared of?' I asked him. 'She might say no?'

Someone beeped at us, and Dad speeded up again. 'Very well then, I'll ask her,' he said.

For a while I sat silent, thinking. What Dad had told me explained a lot. I remembered asking Mum, when I was about 8, why I had no grandparents. Other children had them, and got regular visits, and presents at Christmas.

'You did have grandparents,' Mum told me, 'but they were quite old when you were born, and none of them are still alive.'

That wasn't exactly true, was it, Mum? If you didn't know who your father was, how could you know if he was dead or alive?

I wondered if she had ever tried to find him. Probably not – that wasn't the sort of thing Mum would do. She would rather cover up the fact that she had never known him.

I thought about what it must have been like, growing up at a time when it was a shameful thing to have no father. And how unfair it was to be made to feel second class, not good enough.

There was nothing Mum could do about it, except try harder and harder to win people's approval – for her, and for me. She'd tried to bring me up to be perfectly behaved, so that no one could criticise me. But I hadn't turned out the way she'd hoped.

Would she stop loving me now? I knew Dad never would. He had always loved me, even when I disobeyed him. Like today, when he'd set out to look for me long before I called for help.

That was the best kind of love, I decided. It didn't depend on good behaviour. It was what God's love was supposed to be like, wasn't it?

How do you know that? How will you ever find out, if you keep running in the opposite direction?

This thought made me uneasy. I tried to ignore it by looking out of the window. But there wasn't much to see – we were on the motorway by now. Only darkness, and the endless river of car lights, streaming into the distance.

Dad gave an enormous yawn. 'Talk to me,' he said. 'Otherwise I'm going to fall asleep at the wheel.'

I said, 'Dad, you know when you came looking for me, how were you planning to do it? I could have been anywhere in the whole of London. Or on a train going home. Anywhere at all.'

'True,' he said. 'I could have started driving around aimlessly, but it would have been hard to see you in the dark. I might have driven right past without spotting you. I didn't know what to do, so I prayed. And I felt as if God was telling me: "Just wait. You won't find her until she wants to be found."'

'And then I rang you,' I said, 'and you were only around the corner. I couldn't believe it! Oh, Dad, I was so pleased to see you.'

'Not as pleased as I was to see you. I felt like the father in the Bible, in one of the stories Jesus told. The father whose son ran away but then came back home again. He said, "Let's eat and celebrate. This son of mine was dead, but has now come back to life. He was lost and has now been found."'

'Dad! I was only gone for a day, not years and years.' I knew the story he was talking about. 'And I wasn't exactly homeless and starving, living on pig food.'

'No. I should imagine pig food's quite hard to get hold of in Kensington,' he said, laughing.

Then his voice turned serious. 'Can you remember the meaning of that story?'

Of course I could. I'd only heard it about a thousand times. 'It means God is like a father who loves his children.'

'Yes, and even if they go away from him, he never stops loving them.' He was silent for a minute. Then he said, 'But the runaway son didn't know that for certain. Not until he actually came back to his father. That's when he found out how much he was loved.'

'Like I didn't know you had come all the way to London, looking for me,' I said. 'I only found out when I rang you.'

'Yes, exactly. If you had been too proud or too ashamed to get in touch, where would you be now?'

'Freezing to death in London,' I said. 'Looking for a shop doorway to sleep in, not knowing you were only around the corner.'

Dad said, 'It's like that with God. You can't know the Father's love if you've turned your back on him and keep walking away from him.'

He said nothing more. But I couldn't get his words out of my mind.

Could it be that I had got things all wrong? Knowing God wasn't about keeping a whole lot of rules – I already knew I couldn't do that. It was more about learning to love a Father who already loved me. Who longed for me to come back to him. But who wouldn't find me unless I wanted to be found.

Oh, God... I do want to be found. I'm sorry I went away from you. Please let me come back and be your child again...

Nothing dramatic happened. There was no blinding light, like Paul, the great apostle in the Bible, had seen. I didn't feel any different at all, in fact. Had God heard me? Was he actually there at all?

'Dad,' I said hesitantly, 'when someone comes back to God, should they feel different?'

'Well, some people do. But some don't,' Dad said. 'Not straight away.'

'So, if you don't feel anything, how do you know if God heard you?'

'It doesn't depend on how we feel,' Dad said. He thought for a minute. Then he said, 'When we turn off this motorway onto another one, it won't feel or look any different, apart from the road signs every few miles. We may feel as if nothing's changed – but that won't alter the fact that we'll be heading in a different direction.'

Somehow he seemed to know what I'd just done, although I hadn't been able to put it into words.

He said, 'Jesus made a promise. *I will never turn away anyone who comes to me.* Remember that. Even if you don't feel any different, that was his promise, and you can trust him.'

'Yes.'

I stared out at the road in front, or rather at the long stream of car lights. It was so dark, there was no way of knowing which way we were heading. North, south, east or west? Then a road sign loomed up. *Birton 58*, it said. That was proof that we were travelling in the right direction.

There was still a long way to go. But we were on the right road… going home.

20
Bad publicity

I was really glad that I hadn't told anyone about my plan to escape to London. It would have been awful to have people keep on asking me, 'Well? How did it go on *Starmakers*?'

I did want to know how it had gone, but when I texted Rachel, she didn't answer. I didn't keep on trying to contact her – I'd had enough of doing that. Also, I was getting sick of the word *Starmakers*. It left a nasty taste in my mouth.

By now, I was 90 per cent certain that Rachel had deliberately got me out of the group and replaced me with Keeley. But she'd done it in such a devious way! I wouldn't have minded – correction, I wouldn't have minded so much – if she'd been up front about it. Then I wouldn't have made that wasted journey and lost all my money.

Normally I would have felt angry and bitter. Instead, I actually felt rather sorry for Rachel. She was so desperate to be famous – hungry for it. She would do anything, even stab her friends in the back, because she needed other people's approval so much.

On Friday, when Charlie called for me on the way to school, she was carrying a newspaper. 'Look! Rachel's in the paper!' she said excitedly.

'That's nice.'

'No, it isn't. She's in big trouble – look at this!'

'THE *STARMAKERS* CHEAT', the headline read. There was a picture of Last Minute outside the hotel, with Rachel in the middle, looking downcast.

'Rachel Collins (13) has admitted that she lied and cheated to get on the popular TV show. She pretended to be 16, and told the judges her mother was dying of cancer, to win their sympathy. When the truth was discovered, her group Last Minute was immediately disqualified. The show's producer refused to comment, saying only that everyone should watch *Starmakers* on Saturday night.' There was a lot more, but I didn't bother to read it.

'Rachel will absolutely hate this,' said Charlie, grinning.

'Will she? I'm not so sure,' I said. 'She once said there's no such thing as bad publicity.'

'That's obviously what the producer of *Starmakers* thinks,' Abena said. 'I suppose the viewing figures will double.'

Charlie said, 'Rachel had better be more careful in future. She's famous now.'

She was clearly enjoying the thought of Rachel getting into trouble. And normally I would have been the same. Now, somehow, I didn't feel like gloating. What was happening to me?

On Saturday night, I watched *Starmakers* along with Mum and about ten million other people. The programme had been filmed at the London hotel. On day one, several groups got eliminated, but Last Minute somehow survived into the second day.

Then we saw Rachel being hauled up in front of the judges. First she was questioned about her age, and asked if she could produce proof that she was 16. Obviously she couldn't, and she began to look nervous.

Kate asked about her sick mother. 'What's the matter with her, exactly?'

'Lung cancer,' said Rachel.

'Oh, that's tragic,' said Kate. 'How long has she been ill?'

'It started about... er... six months ago,' said Rachel, looking uncomfortable. 'She gave up smoking but it didn't seem to help.'

Actually, her mum was a health-obsessed doctor, who hated even the smell of cigarettes. But that's the trouble with lying. Once you start, it's like a maze – you have to keep on going, getting further and further in.

'Do you think your mum would like to come and see you perform?' asked Paul. 'We could easily arrange it.'

'She couldn't – she's not well enough,' said Rachel. 'Look, if you don't mind, I'd rather not talk about it. I get too upset...'

'Oh come on, Rachel,' Tony Stewart cut in. 'Be honest. The only thing that upsets you is the thought of being kicked out of the contest. Which we're about to do – because we know you've lied to us from start to finish.'

'We've found out some more about your mother,' said Paul. 'She's a doctor, isn't she? And she's not ill at all. She hasn't had a day off sick in years.'

'You lied to us, Rachel,' Kate said sadly. 'And we believed you.'

Rachel began to cry. The camera zoomed in, recording every single teardrop, to be shown on millions of TVs all across the country.

'That show is dreadful,' said Mum. 'People just get used and then thrown away. I never thought I'd say this, but I actually feel sorry for Rachel.'

I felt the same. I didn't want to watch any more.

****

After I prayed that prayer in the car, I didn't feel any different. But I began to realise that I was changing... or rather, that God had started to change me. There might still be a long way to go – but I was heading in a new direction.

I started to pray more. For ages, my only prayers had been a sort of mumble in church, just meaningless words, so familiar I could say them without thinking. But now the words took on meaning, because I realised God would hear them. And not only in church – any time, day or night, I could talk to my Father.

I surprised my friends by offering to help on the upcoming homeless project. That long evening on a cold street corner had given me a bit of sympathy for homeless people. It must be terrible to live on the streets for weeks, months and years.

Even more amazing – Mum decided to help, too. Dad must have used his famous powers of persuasion. And with Mum's organising skills, the project should soon be up and running.

Dad also managed to get Mum to go and see a doctor, who told her she might have a thyroid problem. 'That's what could be making me feel so tired and depressed,' she said. 'I thought it was my age, or the move to the city. I believed it was something I would just have to put up with. But I'm going to try out these pills and see what happens.'

I don't think it's the pills that are making her feel better, though. I think it's because she and Dad are talking again. And she's definitely mellowed a bit towards me. (Dad must have had a word with her, like he promised.) She actually let me go to a party last week, without too much fuss. And she let me choose the frames for my new glasses, when we replaced the ones that were stolen.

I think she's given up the attempt to turn me into the perfect vicar's daughter. In return, I am trying not to be so much of a rebel. That's only fair. I just wish I could get her to call me Emma instead of Eunice, but after 14 years, that might be too much to ask.

Still, she does realise I'm growing up. She's trying not to treat me like a little kid. The other day, when she asked what I wanted for my birthday, I said I'd like to have my own TV in my room. 'I could pay for part of it,' I said, although I knew it wasn't really the cost that worried her. It was the thought that I might watch something she didn't approve of.

She hesitated. At first I was sure she would refuse. Then she said, 'I'll see what your father thinks.'

'OK.'

This was progress! No long arguments and no sulking on my part. No *no means no* from Mum.

She said, 'But if you do get one, promise me one thing, Eun... Emma.'

What was coming now? Don't watch it after 9pm? Only watch nature programmes? On second thoughts, nature programmes could be a bit risky...

'Don't watch that *Starmakers* programme,' she said.

'I won't,' I said. 'I promise.'

****

On Saturday night, I went to the cinema with Charlie and Abena. Afterwards, as we waited outside for Mum to pick us up, I began to hear music. It was coming from a nearby pub, which had a sign outside: *LIVE MUSIC TONITE!*

And what was that name scribbled underneath?

Last Minute
As seen on TV
Admission Free

This I had to see. I strolled along the street and glanced through the window. The pub was half empty, although it was Saturday night. On a small stage in the corner, I saw Lauren and Keeley, along with a keyboard player who looked as if he might be Keeley's brother.

As a group, they didn't sound too bad. They weren't wonderful, either. But that didn't matter because no one seemed to be listening. The customers were talking, drinking and playing darts, pretty well ignoring the music.

'And now we'll sing the song that got us on TV,' Lauren announced. She had a fixed smile on her face, like a bad comedian trying to please a difficult audience. 'Here it is… "Summertime".'

A few people listened for a minute or two, then carried on with their conversations. It was quite obvious that Lauren and Keeley didn't have star quality, whatever that might be. Not like Rachel. But then Rachel had ruined her chance.

Abena and Charlie came to join me. 'What's going on?' Charlie asked.

'Look. It's Last Minute,' I said. 'Making the most of their last minutes of fame.'

We watched them for a while. 'That is so sad,' said Charlie. 'Somebody should tell them they're never going to make it to Number One.'

'And even if they did, it wouldn't make them happy,' said Abena.

'Yeah, yeah. Being famous doesn't make people happy,' said Charlie. 'You keep saying that.'

'Never mind being famous. Just *wanting* to be famous can screw people's lives up,' I said. 'Like Rachel's, for instance.'

We walked back towards the cinema. (It would not be a good move to have Mum arrive and find us hanging around outside the pub.)

Charlie said, 'I wonder if Rachel will ever get to be famous. I mean, *really* famous. I always thought she could be a pretty good actress if she tried.'

I looked at the posters outside the cinema, imagining Rachel's name up there. *Naked Ambition, starring Rachel Collins.*

Abena said, 'Yes. Ten years from now we might be telling people that we used to know her when she was a kid.'

'And they won't believe us,' said Charlie.

I said, 'I sort of hope she does get to be famous. I hope she gets everything she wants. You know – fame and money and attention. Arriving at premieres in a stretch limo. Getting invites to all the right parties.'

'Why?' Charlie demanded.

But Abena understood. 'Unless she gets what she thinks she wants, she won't realise that it isn't what she *really* wants.'

'Don't try to confuse me,' said Charlie. 'Emma, where's your mum? I wish she'd hurry up. I'm freezing.'

'Me too,' said Abena, shivering. 'Hey, there's one thing I'd like if I was famous. Not the money and the parties and all that. Just give me the chauffeur-driven limo.'

'And here it is,' I said, as the car rolled up. 'One silver limo, cunningly disguised as a Fiat Uno. Chauffeur-driven by my mum.'

Abena sighed. 'I suppose it will have to do. At least the paparazzi will never spot us. Come on then – let's go.'

Abena thought she was beginning to sort her life out. She had made the huge step of becoming a Christian – a real Christian, not just a person who happens to go to church – and she'd finally broken free of Rachel's clutches. But a chance meeting with a boy from her home country in West Africa throws all of that into confusion. Now the lessons she has been learning about trusting God and forgiving others (like Rachel) are in danger of being forgotten all together.

Read Abena's story in

No Love Lost

The sequel to *No Means No* and *No Angel*.